To our friend Kitty!

Alton R Barnes

Silent Courage

by Alton Roscoe Barnes

ISBN-10: 1-4392-1945-1

EAN-13: 978-1-4392-1945-4

Interior formatting/cover design by

Rend Graphics 2008

www.rendgraphics.com

Published by:

BookSurge Publishing

www.booksurge.com

Silent Courage

Silent Courage

Introduction

The sound of a ringing telephone in the dead of night can bring fear to your soul. Man must have a built-in alarm system that senses tragedy before it happens. During the Great War, German Jews must have sensed danger when German Soldiers came knocking at night. They had no choice but to open their doors to them. The poor souls must have trembled.

John Randall, the subject of this story, must have witnessed this kind of fear learning personal lessons from his war experiences. The man displayed great courage facing his fears head on, accepting the hard knocks life dealt him. His metal was tested not only in war, but what he faced later in his life.

I am Gerald Price, Jr. My wife once called me at the office late at night. I must admit it upset me for a moment. Megan knew working late wasn't my nature. I actually lied to her and I'm not sure why. The truth is, I lost track of time. Time is a precious gift to each of us. We only have so much of it. It comes and goes like a gust of wind, here one moment then gone forever. There is a fact about time; people find enough of it to do things they consider enjoyable. Such is the case with me at the moment. I enjoy writing. I once wanted to make writing my life's vocation, but Mother insisted I study law, so each day I strike juries, spend hours in research or in the courtroom. I could write books about the law, but my aim is to acquaint you with my friend, John Randall.

John spent time in what we might say was literally hell. He lived on life's edge through moments most of us will never encounter. If strength of character is the measure of a man, then John Randall is a giant. His graying hair and scarred face are not signs of aging, but badges of courage. John served as an infantry soldier during the Korean War. He wasn't a George Patton or Dwight D. Eisenhower or an Audi Murphy or Sergeant York, but he could have been.

I met John in August 1981. He came to visit my grandparents near the cotton mill town of Morrisville. I grew up nearby on Nolen's Ranch.

Activity in small southern towns near the beginning of the Industrial Revolution centered round textile cotton mills. There are still large cotton growing plantations in the south. As a youngster, I never knew much about textile mills, but I learned to appreciate the process of taking cotton from the fields, sending it through several procedures to develop it into cloth. The hum of Morrisville's cotton mill still lingers in my mind. When I close my eyes, I can see hundreds of men and women at work in that mill, earning weekly wages, weaving cotton into twine. The sound of the town's cotton gin during harvesting season still lingers with me; that special never ceasing whine was unique. For weeks the gin's suction system would inhale cotton from horse drawn wagons, and the gin would separate the lent from the seeds. I spent hours watching ole Ely's masterpiece crank out those large bales that would wind up at the mill.

How the town functioned is phenomenal. Morrisville had no mayor, city council or city government. The mill's superintendent was sole authority; the commander in chief with power to hire and fire. The owners placed confidence in the man. They provided a band for the community's recreational pleasure, a basketball and a baseball team as well. Afternoons and most evenings, the band would practice. The loud, often screechy noise from trainees trying to learn to play, scattered far and wide bringing frowns and sometimes laughter to the community, but they learned music.

Morrisville was small. A census of every Negro, Caucasian, man, woman, and child, might have approached a thousand.

Out from Morrisville was a place known as Rocky Mount. My grandparents owned a small farm in that community; that's where I first met John.

John Randall once told me of serving in combat with my Father. I've never doubted John's combat experiences in the Korean War. His scars attest to his experience. I've known him for years, but there are times when I question if I've ever known John at all...

For almost thirty years after the Korean War, John lived in Tokyo. I imagine if he had known what he would face when he returned to America, he might have stayed in Japan.

Allow me to share with you this man's silent courage...

Chapter 1

Late June, 1981...

The clouds over Tokyo hung heavy, rain had drenched, the area leaving a strange glow from a rainbow. John Randall called on his old friend near nightfall. His unexpected announcement took Dr. Anoka Faureta by surprise. Anoka, a well known physical therapist practicing in Tokyo held John Randall in high esteem. The Japanese doctor as best he could, covered his displeasure at the announcement, but John knew him too well. His weak attempt failed miserably. Anoka was like a part of John's own body; an open book; they had been friends for years. Anoka stared at his tea on the table; his mind wrestled with the thought of John leaving. Why would John, a happy level headed well trained physical therapist consider giving up his status in Tokyo? It didn't make good sense.

Anoka sat in silence; one sock on, the other barely hanging; the table before him so low he couldn't hide his feet underneath. He removed both socks, crossed his legs to comfort himself, his gray head lowered. He motioned John to sit; John did his bidding. Anoka called the housekeeper to bring John hot tea.

He looked up for the first time. "Remember when we first met, John?"

John nodded, "I remember well, so many years have passed."

Anoka couldn't force himself to look at John a second time or at least he wouldn't. Sitting at Anoka's table was like sitting at his own. John swallowed hard. Anoka's action hurt; he wasn't a surprise.

Taking a deep breath, Anoka sipped the tea; his eyes watered, he coughed.

They'd been close since the Korean War. Anoka cleared his throat, attempted to speak in a soft voice, "It was chilly in October. Yeah, the medics brought you to emergency room. Do you recall?" Anoka asked a slight smile appearing on his bearded face.

John nodded recalling his dilemma. "Yes, I recall."

"You were in shock."

"I know. I couldn't remember that damn North Korean flamethrower."

Anoka reminded him why; he was incoherent. "Friend, you were not expected to survive." Anoka personally treated him for months.

They talked at length for hours about their

friendship, their lives together. John's mind absorbed the thoughts. "Thank you, Anoka, for bringing me through my darkest days."

Their relationship had grown through the years. Anoka looked up; setting his tea own the table. "Remember my counseling? John, it's like I've told you many times, friendship gels in human minds. It gleans forgiveness, and inspires respect, when respect is deserved."

John acknowledged Anoka's comment realizing they were more than friends; Anoka was like his own father.

The last week of June, 1981, John loaded his B-4 bag; the one thing he had retained from military service. He caught a cab to the dock in Yokohama Bay. Thousands of people were already in line virtually pushing and shoving to board the USS Sea Star by 9:00 AM. The ship's captain gave command for the ship to maneuver away from the dock. Those aboard waved their last goodbyes doubting they would see the Island of Honchu again. By evening the ship was well underway. The vessel bounced along the Pacific's high waves, a soothing gentle breeze blew across its worn, but well kept weather decks. John watched the busy crew going about their daily chores displaying evidence of the navy's pride. Crew members were quick to relate stories of how the ship had weathered the pacific storms since her launching before the beginning of World War II. John smiled at an instant thought that entered his mind. If the old warrior could speak she would tell stories of how she and her crews had transported army brigades into war zones.

After weeks at sea, late in the evening, John stood on deck, his eyes fixed on the waters below with an urge to jump, end it all, the thought came to his mind. But Anoka would say rational human beings never commit suicide; that's an act of the sick or insane. Anoka would advise to concentrate on one thing at a time. At the moment, he was going home, that thought was sufficient, nothing else should matter. But then his mind settled on seagulls dipping their beaks well below the sea water's surface, mountain size waves rolled in toward the ship's bow. The fine mist felt good to his scarred face. He thought of himself as a hitch hiker, authorized military travel by ship when space was available. The military had been good to him; retired pay had kept him afloat for years.

Checking his Timex, it was getting late. The boatswain's whistle would sound any minute now declaring lights out on all weather decks. He marveled at this mode of communication, a system developed he knew not when that gave commanders a quick way to send messages to his crew. The skinny young sailor took pride in blowing his whistle; a routine the sailor had followed every day and night since the ship left Japan. Suddenly, the boatswain's blast said plainly clear the ship's top deck.

John first looked toward the bow; then toward the stern; other passengers had long since gone inside; a few sailors remained top side. He thought of Faureta. He would have enjoyed this trip, but the old man hardly ever traveled outside Tokyo. He certainly wouldn't think of leaving Japan. A trip to the states was out of the question. But Anoka's thinking was rational. After all, Anoka had turned eighty years of age.

John turned to re-enter the ship's quarters; flipped the remainder of his cigarette overboard before taking a last look at the horizon. They'd arrive in Hawaii by morning.

He started for the lounge, but thought better of it. A drink would only dull his senses, not quench his thirst nor prevent the pestering visions. He questioned his judgment of returning home. At forty eight, he had only a vague memory of the states. His mind kept saying life did not begin at the foot of a Korean mountainside; there had to be more, but he wasn't sure. Visions popped into his head, uninvited...a ship would land; the wind carried an odor, then a beach would appear; waves rushed in sending foam shoreward. The water would dissipate into sand carrying with it small sand crabs. There must be a way to clear his cloudy mind.

The boatswain's whistle sounded a second time. John lay staring at the ceiling, the ship pitched, his mind rambled. Every conceivable emotion poured like a fountain into his brain. Then he struggled with his memory. Did he actually have a wife? If so, would she be waiting after so many years? A woman in her right mind wouldn't wait forever. Any wife would have long since declared him dead. There had to be a purpose for his survival, but for what reason? The military's plan for his recovery had not failed nor completely succeeded. But for sure, Anoka had been his salvation. So far, life, except for the visions was normal. He'd spent more time in therapy than he cared to recall. Faureta, bless his soul, had indoctrinated him well. Before Anoka's counsel, he recalled burying himself in books. Anoka approved, but at times, the old shit could irritate his own mother. "Randall," he would say, "Do you think you're the only scar faced man on the planet? My friend, Doctor Hanaoka dedicated his life to studying medicine. Don't be so self centered. Hanaoki never thought of himself." John thought of Faureta, wished he would have come along. The old man would say. "Hanaoki spent his life developing techniques to help people like you."

He wondered about tomorrow, but for now, he'd get some rest.

After breakfast, sailors buzzed the ship's deck like bees gathering honey, cleaning fore and aft. Seagulls swarmed like darting insects around the ship's fantail picking up crumbs tossed overboard by kitchen police. At a distance John spotted the Hawaiian Islands. Blue colored mountains seemed to rise from the ocean floor then descend again when large waves rushed toward the ship's bow. John's mind captured the image of an unforgettable mountainside that haunted him to tear. There came chanting screams from North Koreans advancing down a mountainside. The sounds lingered. Pressing his hands against his ears didn't stop the sound. Maybe if he could find his family, if in truth he had one, be surrounded by loved ones. Maybe these visions would subside; leave forever.

Standing on desk, looking into the morning sun, for a moment John felt his full memory had returned. He recalled a tall soldier tossing him a rifle. Suddenly, pain penetrated his temples; his memory failed. Where had time gone?

A familiar voice from behind called his name. Jeff Collier was approaching. What was Jeff doing on board? Jeff yawned, covering his eyes from the morning sun. "You're out early, ole man." Jeff grinned.

John, raising an arm to block the sun, "Old man?" John laughed, "I didn't know you were aboard." John flipped a half burned cigarette into the waters. "Your wife with you?"

"No, Sarah hates to travel." He looked at the waves crashing into the ship's side.

"Think they'll let us off?"

"Doubt it. We'll see."

The ship churned into the harbor; wake rushing shoreward. The Captain came on the intercom. "Debark if you like, but be back on board in thirty minutes. The time is 1022 hours."

John and Jeff decided to walk to a nearby restaurant for coffee. They sat outside, a salty breeze blowing in from the Pacific. The Arizona Memorial stood in the bay; a reminder of World War II. John turned his scarred face; stretched a frown, showing minor interest in the Arizona.

Jeff paused, looking at John. The two had known each other for years. They had shared the same apartment complex in downtown Tokyo. "Going home for a visit?" Jeff asked.

John gazed across the waters. "Not sure. I don't know much about home."

Jeff frowned, a smile appeared. "Are you serious?"

John nodded his head. "Yes, I'm serious." He checked his watch. "It's time we return."

Walking back, John sensed he had been abrupt. "Jeff, I was wounded in the war. My records show I'm from Columbus, Georgia, but I have no recollection of Columbus or a family." John related his strange visions; seeing a teenage boy playing on a mountainside. Occasionally, a woman appeared. She beckoned, but never called his name. Once he saw a small town near railroad tracks. He heard the grind of a mill; smelled the scent of hamburgers. Then he felt the flame thrower....

Jeff led the way up the gang plank. On deck they determined only a few had left the ship. Moments later, the captain declared the vessel underway. John mentioned an army buddy, Gerald Price, but Jeff reminded him he was not a soldier. He came to Japan to teach school at a military installation.

Like new falling snow blankets the mountains of Alaska, the morning fog spread over San Francisco Bay. The Sea Star remained at a distance from shore; waiting for day to break. Below, the smell of bacon frying announced the kitchen crew was preparing breakfast for passengers before they debarked. Jeff crawled from his bunk, rushed to take a leak, took a quick shower, brushed his teeth, combed his thinning hair and went to the kitchen. John had already arrived. They sat making small talk until an army private offered them a cup of coffee.

Near mid morning the captain gave debarkation instructions. John and Jeff, gathered their luggage and walked down the gangplank to the dock below; Jeff stretched his arms above his head; John, lit his last cigarette. They walked to a small restaurant a few blocks away. In the restaurant Jeff sensed the reality of John's problem. Trauma had affected the man's mind.

Before noon, John took a cab to the airport, found the

Delta counter, and purchased a ticket to Birmingham. Soon a female voice on intercom gave boarding instructions. A voice inside John's head was saying, "Go to Columbus." However, his sense of judgment said, "Go by Sylacauga." Why Sylacauga? Gerald Price must have mentioned Sylacauga. Otherwise, how would he know of the place?

In late afternoon, Delta's flight from Atlanta arrived at the Birmingham airport. John retrieved his luggage and hailed a taxi to take him to the downtown bus station. Again, thoughts of his family surfaced, but he pushed them to the back of his mind. He must have parents someplace, dead or alive. Every person was born with a mother and father; he was no different. His military papers mentioned dependents. Anoka would say, "John, worry is not the answer." At the bus station he purchased a ticket to Sylacauga. Why Sylacauga? The thought warmed his heart. Gerald once told him he lived there. It had to be Gerald who told him or how else would he know? He wouldn't resist the urge to go. He must go to Sylacauga.

Chapter 2

July 1981....

Birmingham Southern College's campus hummed with young and old from, not only Alabama, but other states as well. This was graduation day at the four year Liberal Arts College. The ceremony would begin at 11:00 AM.

By 9:00 AM, Birmingham's down town traffic was beginning to gain momentum. People from the rural areas flooded into the downtown area to do their weekly shopping. On this particular Saturday morning crowds of teenagers were lined along the street waiting to see a movie at the Alabama Theater. The sweltering July sun showed no mercy. Its rays beamed downward, heating the paved streets and concrete sidewalks. With little or no air stirring, the morning dew turned into steam that scalded the faces of downtown visitors. Sweat poured from people, drenching their clothing as they hurried along the busy streets, eager to finish their shopping, more eager to take leave from the sweltering heat.

Megan Scott, walked from her dorm's parlor to the long porch which extended the length of the dormitory. Birmingham Southern, built in the early part of the twentieth century, stands on rolling hills in northwest Birmingham. The school, for years was the religious training ground for Methodist Ministers, as well as, several other liberal arts.

Megan decided to wait on the steps for her mother who would be driving up from Montgomery. She tingled inside at the thought of what this day meant to her. It had been a long four years, but with graduation in sight, it was worth the effort.

Megan sat with several other students waiting to welcome their guests. Looking toward the school's main entrance, she recognized Dot's car pulling into the parking lot. Dot Sutton locked her car, and hurried crossed the street. Megan jumped to her feet, mother and daughter hurried to embrace each other. Megan never mentioned her feelings to a soul, and certainly not to her mother, but she was proud of Dot's youthful appearance. Dot, at fifty, could pose as a much younger woman. Megan secretly wished her father could be present, but dared not divulge her thoughts to her mother. The divorce two years after Megan was born had been bitter, leaving scars Dot wouldn't talk about. Lonnie Sutton left her to care for their two year old. Dot's life since the divorce had not been easy, but she gave Megan an education.

As Megan grew up, mother and daughter learned to accept their life without Lonnie. Dot for years managed in her small Montgomery apartment. Now she could boast that Megan had earned top honors.

At 9:30 AM Gerald Price's telephone rang; the secretary called, "It's for you, Mr. Price."

Megan reminded him of his promise. "You will be here, won't you?"

"Yes, Meg, I'll leave in a few."

Before 11:00 AM, Gerald arrived; Megan and Dot were waiting on the steps. Megan's announcement could wait until an appropriate time.

When Gerald proposed marriage, he quickly let Megan know he cared not for a large church wedding. Reared on a ranch near Morrisville, Gerald Price was known not to care for social aspects of city life. His law practice required him to live in an apartment in Birmingham, but he sorely missed the soothing smell of the ranch in early spring, the freshness of newly plowed ground, the lowing of cattle in the evenings, the quietness of twilight time, the singing of the katydids and the flashing lights of the fire flies. Gerald tried to talk Megan into purchasing a home in the mountains of south Birmingham, the hill country near the Vulcan monument, but Megan preferred to rent until she could settle into her job with the Birmingham News. She'd never worked for a newspaper, but her father once was editor of the Montgomery Advertiser. To be a newspaper woman had been her life's ambition. But now that she had finished her degree in journalism, she wasn't excited about going to work.

At 11:00 AM the ceremony began, following the same format of graduations in the past. Soon as it ended, Gerald suggested they go to lunch downtown. The restaurant was packed and it seemed to take forever to be served. After lunch, Gerald left them in the parking lot and hurried back to the office knowing he had taken more time than anticipated. Jim Berry, an older lawyer with the firm, the only other firm member working on Saturday, met him at the door. "It's time you get your butt to work." Jim's red face was the man's trade mark. Gerald, a junior firm member, resented his remark, but knew better than to comment. He'd learned early on to not tangle with the older attorneys. Members of the firm thought Berry set a good example; Gerald's conception was different. Berry was known as one of Birmingham's best lawyers, but the man was a workaholic. Gerald refused to take work home.

Two days later....

Gerald, busy in research received a telephone call. Megan wanted to say goodbye before leaving to visit her former roommate in New Orleans. She needed time to think through their wedding plans. Sally Landers lived in an apartment near New Orleans' French quarters.

Friday afternoon, Megan sat reading a novel when Delta called her flight; she boarded, sat near a window. Soon after take off she fell asleep, didn't awake until the pilot announced, "Seat belts on." In the shadows of the waiting room, Sally Landers waited. Sally rushed to embrace Megan before they moved to the baggage room to retrieve her luggage.

Sally's apartment was filled with evidence of her stressful job, stacks of law books and papers everywhere. Sally had gone to work for a New Orleans Legal firm, a job she only tolerated. Megan felt her frustration, but chose to wait, almost ashamed, to talk about her own displeasure with the reporter's job. The two talked of college days; the highlights they had experienced, as well as, the valleys they had crossed together. Neither had found journalism to their liking. Sally continued to work, but had enrolled in medical school. "Megan, I can't take this legal crap much longer."

Megan nodded. "So, you're back in school? Your parents help with tuition?"

"Yes, if I need it." Sally moved to the kitchen to start dinner; Megan followed close behind. Little did they know what their futures held; an illness for one that neither expected. It would bring stress to a close friendship that both had cherished through college. Their wants, desires, attitudes toward life were quickly changing.

Near mid-might, they went to their own bedroom.

Sally not sure if she had ever known the girl in the other room; Megan's feelings were similar. Megan decided to tough out the week, but she would cut the visit short.

Monday morning, Sally's alarm clock rocked the room at 6:00 AM. Sally ate a light breakfast before leaving for class. She left Megan asleep. Near nine, Megan awaked, a strange feeling obsessed her; someone was in her room. Fear crept inside her body. She sat up, her heart pounding; perspiration formed on her brow. She looked at her trembling hands; got out of bed, ran to the mirror. Something was different. Something inside her body tugged at her. She returned to bed expecting the feeling to subside; it didn't.

Someone screamed. She recognized the voice, her own; she was actually screaming, but why? Someone appeared, a woman. The door to the bedroom slammed. She had slammed the door. Megan thought of shaking the door, but couldn't move. Was she losing her mind? Blood drained from her face. She wrestled with her emotions; she was having a bad dream. No, it was no dream. Was she dying? No, she was too young to die. Why would a woman want to lock her in the room? In the mirror on the bathroom door, the woman's image appeared again. She felt relieved, no need to worry. The woman she saw in the mirror was her own being, but something was different. She couldn't speak her name. With eyes fixed on the female, Megan watched the woman's image fade. Now she could speak; she was Megan, no one else was in the room. She was Megan Sutton from Birmingham, Alabama. Frightened at the thought, she again questioned her own sanity. Without warning, it happened again. She felt her whole self fading....

The blond figure went through Sally's closet, found a flimsy costume Sally had worn to celebrate Mardi Gras. She quickly dressed, put on heavy make-up, painted on loads of lipstick; saturated her body with perfume. The cab driver dropped her off in the French Quarters and she walked alone through the shops. Her sexy look caught the eye of a lone visitor, a man dressed in western attire. He invited her to join him for a cup of tea. He pointed toward a small sidewalk café across the street; moments later, he placed their order.

"What brings you to New Orleans?" he asked.

Her eyes pierced his. "Do I look like a visitor?"

The man laughed, his mind struggling to understand. Maybe she was an undercover agent. "Sorry, but I'm a visitor and I assumed you were."

She sipped the tea, laughed. "Well, I'm not from New Orleans. I'm visiting a friend."

The man nodded, "May I ask your name?"

"Melanie."

"Melanie, I'm Stanley Wilson from Arizona."

"Arizona?" She laughed, nodding her head. "You must be here alone."

Wilson nodded. "I am and my friends call me Stan." He kept his eyes directly on hers. She was beautiful, all right, but strange.

Melanie looked across the street, a Mime was performing his act; people had gathered. She turned her attention to Stanley. "Arizona? No, I'm not interested in your part of the world." She smiled, "I have to go. Someone is waiting for me."

"Wait. You didn't tell me where you live?" He laughed.

"No, I didn't, did I?"

At 2:00 PM, Sally's classes ended. She drove home expecting to find Megan ready to visit a part of the city. Megan wasn't there. Sally assumed she went shopping. She decided to prepare dinner and await Megan's return. Near 5:30 PM, the doorbell rang. Sally looked into Megan's eyes. It was Megan Scott all right, but Sally couldn't believe Megan was dressed in her Mardi Gras clothes. What was happening to the Megan Scott she had known in college? The Megan who stood before her was a stranger. Megan went to the living room and plopped on the couch, her short dress, exposing her legs.

Sally's concern mounted. This woman wasn't the roommate she had known in college. "Megan, what gives? Where have you been?"

The woman on the couch laughed, "Megan? I'm not Megan, honey. Why should you have the audacity to ask where I've been? You're not my keeper, and who are you?" Melanie asked.

Sally's concern mounted; now, not only for her friend Megan, but for her own safety --she felt chills. The woman on the couch was definitely not Megan Scott. She looked like Megan, had Megan's voice, but she couldn't be Megan. Sally decided that her best bet at the moment was to go along and not upset the woman in Megan's body. She prepared a cup of tea and brought it to the living room.

The woman on the couch laughed, "Thanks, but I don't drink tea. Do you have a martini?"

Sally felt sick. Megan Scott never touched alcohol. In utter confusion, Sally shouted. "Megan Scott, please cut the crap. What are you trying to pull?"

Melanie laughed, "Don't call me...Megan. I don't care for that bitch." She slurred. "Yeah, that's what she is, a mean bitch. And who are you?" Melanie asked.

Sally's anger mounted, "Come on, Megan, please... cut the act."

Melanie, jumped to her feet, slinging a pillow against the wall, "Look, lady I'm not Megan." Melanie moved to the front door and pounded it with her fist. "I'm so sick of being called by that name."

Sally, frustrated, said no more, turned on the TV. If Megan kept up the act, she'd ask her to leave tomorrow.

Melanie went to the kitchen, opened the refrigerator, took out a coke and came to the couch. Without comment, she set the coke on the end table; lay down on the couch and within minutes, fell asleep. Sally covered her body, wondering what was happening to Megan's mind. Megan slept until after 8:00 PM.

Suddenly, Megan sat up and asked Sally what they were having for dinner. Sally moved to Megan's side. "Are you there, Megan?" Sally asked.

Looking puzzled, she marveled at Sally's concern, a frown appearing. "Sally, what gives?"

Sally smiled, getting up from the couch, "You slept so soundly." She moved to the kitchen to prepare Megan a plate. After dinner, Megan helped with the dishes. "Sally, I'm going home in the morning. It seems we haven't had much time together."

"We haven't, Megan. I came home expecting to take you out on the town...."

Megan frowned, "I don't recall you suggesting we go, Sally. I'm sorry if I have been rude."

Sally looked into Megan's frustrated eyes. It was obvious, Meg wasn't well. After dinner, they watched television until bedtime. In the privacy of her bedroom, Sally picked up the telephone receiver....

Chapter 3

Third week in July....

Gerald waited several days, not convinced he should discuss Megan's behavior with his mother, not sure he shouldn't. She could provide insight, but on second thought, why should he involve his mother in his personal affairs? He'd wait till he observed Megan's behavior himself. If Meg was ill, she could find medical help in Birmingham. He thought of Megan's quick mind. She'd be okay once she had sufficient rest. Her behavior had to be stress related.

Friday evening near sundown, Megan's plane landed at the Birmingham airport. Several passengers hurried to retrieve their baggage. Stanley Wilson stepped into the coffee shop; waited till Megan retrieved her luggage. Stepping to the outside, she located a taxi; Stanley took a second one. Megan's driver drove southeast to her apartment. Stanley's driver followed. He returned downtown and checked into a motel. He decided to wait until Monday to return to Arizona.

Megan unpacked, prepared a light dinner, took a bath and went straight to bed. She felt exhausted, couldn't explain why. Gerald waited for her to call to tell him she was home, but no call came. He rationalized Meg had either decided to stay another night in New Orleans or she had missed her flight.

Monday morning, Gerald dressed, ate a light breakfast and headed for the office. Meg must still be in New Orleans, but why hadn't she called? Sally's comments came to his mind.

Megan waked early, crawled from bed, dressed, ate breakfast and before 8:00 AM she reported to the editor of the Birmingham News. By day's end she was miserable. Writing a society page for a newspaper wasn't as glamorous as she had dreamed. When the day ended, she left the Birmingham News office practically in tears.

At 10:30 AM, Gerald dialed her home; no one answered. He'd try again later in the day.

Monday evening she decided to keep her problem to herself; sleep on what she had to do.

Gerald called, they chatted. She claimed to be tired and ended the conservation, took a bath, went to bed early.

Tuesday morning she dressed for work. Dreading the thought of going to the office, she forced herself to go. She arrived before 8:00 AM, pulled into the parking lot, sat for a few minutes, cranked up and returned home.

Tuesday evening she called her mother. Dot Sutton was furious. "Megan, you've left your job without giving yourself a chance to like it."

Dot's screams fell on deaf ears; Megan had heard those screams as a child. "I don't need this, Mamma." She shouted. "Good night!"

"But, Megan, you're acting like a child." Megan had hung up.

Megan fell across her bed. Filled with frustration and anger, she softly wept promising herself never to seek work as a journalist again. Gerald called; she let the phone ring, debated if she should answer. She picked up the receiver.

She recognized his voice. "Hi, how was your day?" Gerald asked.

She hedged, "Filled with troubles." She laughed. "I'll explain later."

After a short chat, she suddenly developed a sick headache and hung up. Gerald thought about Sally's comments.

Wednesday morning at 10:00 AM, Gerald's telephone rang.

"Could we have lunch today?" Megan asked.

Gerald, busy in research, cut the conversation short. He would meet her by 12:15 PM at Britney's.

At 11:45 AM Megan pulled into Britney's parking lot, went inside and waited... At 12 o'clock, Gerald came through the door. They went through the line and located a table near the front.

Gerald eyed her, "Okay, Meg, what gives?"

Megan dabbed the corner of her eyes, "I no longer work for the Birmingham News. Journalism isn't for me."

Gerald shook his head, a frown appeared. "You're a journalism graduate, Megan. You haven't given yourself a chance." He looked out the window, then into her eyes. "What are you going to do?"

She frowned. "Not sure," she shrugged "but I'm no journalist."

Gerald, disappointed, but compassionate, "Okay, Mother has influential friends. Should we ask her to help?"

"You will not, Gerald Price. Only weak wimps run to their mother for help."

"I'm no wimp, Megan. Mother has friends over here in high places."

"It's not your mother's problem, it's mine."

First week August....

Megan took a job at a textile plant as a company payroll clerk. The job was menial, absent of responsibility. She was pleased; so was Gerald. It made Gerald's life more bearable. By month's end Megan and Dot finished arrangements for the wedding.

Sylacauga's First Baptist Church was packed. The wedding ceremony was short, but touching. The newlyweds left immediately after the reception and traveled by automobile to New Orleans. Nolen and Sheila Garcia gave them use of the family estate on Lake Ponchartrain for a week as a wedding present.

In late October 1981 Gerald purchased a home in the foothills of Red Mountain. The couple spent time decorating and landscaping the yard. Megan loved the place. She had difficulty leaving it for work each day. Gerald's law practice began to grow requiring more and more of his time. He refused to become a workaholic, a clone of Jim Berry.

Two weeks before Christmas, Gerald came home to find Megan crying. She couldn't explain her mood change. Gerald couldn't conceive of her job causing such a problem.

"Not feeling well, Meg?"

"I'm not sick, Gerald. I hurt within my soul." It was a feeling Megan couldn't explain. Gerald comforted her for several days, thinking of Sally's assessment of Megan's Mobile visit. If Megan had a problem, she must see a doctor. He'd wait for a few more days.

Christmas was only a week away. Gerald dressed and left for work. Megan called in sick. By mid morning, she became obsessed with strange feelings. She suddenly was drifting into a deep hole. A woman appeared. Megan felt helpless, shut into a strange world. Why did this woman look so much like her? The woman was somehow making her a prisoner within her own body.

Melanie dressed in a mini skirt, put on heavy cosmetics, combed her hair over her eyes. She drove Meg's car to the slums of Birmingham, located an open bar. The only participants were several alcoholics. Melanie's entrance gained their attention. She moved directly to the bar, sat on a bar stool and ordered a martini. Moments later, a man appeared at her side. He ordered a beer; stared at Melanie in the mirror above the bar. She smiled, pushing her hair from her eyes.

"I'm Lonnie. Would you allow me to buy you another?"

Melanie laughed, throwing her head back, the alcohol taking effect.

The bartender brought her a second martini. Lonnie backed away. He sensed Melanie was obviously trouble. She turned on her stool toward him, but he left the bar.

Someone put money in the juke box. Hank William's, *I can't stop loving you* began to play. Melanie went to the small dance floor. She began to dance alone, swaying her hips provocatively. The men began to cheer her, she loved their attention.

Gerald arrived home, expecting dinner to be on the table. Instead he found himself alone. Megan hadn't called to say she would be away. His immediate thought rallied to Sally's remarks. In the kitchen he heated a bowl of chicken soup deciding to wait a while, not panic. She could be out buying groceries or taking clothes to the laundry. Then she could be visiting a friend. What the hell, he wouldn't panic. After he had soup for dinner, he poured a glass of wine, went to the den and turned on the television. The wine relaxed his tired mind; he fell asleep in his chair.

The living room clock struck midnight; Gerald waked; Megan had not returned. Panic struck, but he kept his composure. He called the Birmingham Police Department.

He sat in the den waiting, every conceivable scenario played through his mind. Megan could have had an accident, met with tragedy, lying dead in a shallow grave. His disciplined world had taught him worry had its way of seizing the moment, this was such a moment. He kept his mind busy playing solitary, never winning, but the game kept his hands busy. The clock in the living room struck 1:15 AM. The police had to call any moment. Time passed; no calls came from the police. The clock struck again. It was now 3:30 AM, a car pulled into the driveway. He rushed to the window thinking it might be the police; it was Megan. She came up the front steps with key in hand to open the door. Gerald opened it instead. He stood for a long moment, looking at her, the way she was dressed, the glassy eyes, the smell of stale smoke permeated her. "Meg, do you realize what time it is? I have the Birmingham Police looking for you."

"Meg? Gerald Price, I've hated you forever. I'm not Meg." My name is Melanie and I don't care to be called... Meg." She plopped down on the couch, exposing her legs; taking a cigarette from her purse. Gerald knew this was uncharacteristic of Megan.

Gerald, startled at her behavior, concluded he wasn't in the presence of Megan, but she was Megan. She wore Megan's wedding band.

The stranger sitting on the couch got up and moved into the kitchen –Gerald followed. "Meg, go sit in the den and I'll prepare you something to eat."

With a smirk on her face, Melanie lashed out, "I'm not helpless, Gerald." She looked at him, eyes blazing, "I've never cared for you, Gerald!"

Gerald felt hurt, but kept calm, "Okay, Megan, what, do you want of me?"

"First, you may quit calling me, Megan!"

Gerald moved to the den. Melanie plopped on the couch again, placing a pillow under her head. He'd keep quiet, bide his time, not irritate her, note this woman's reactions, wonder what would be her next move? He'd make notes on her behavior when he arrived at the office. Megan said nothing; soon fell asleep.

Near 4:00 AM, Gerald entered his bedroom, called his mother. Thoughts of Megan's mental state kept him awake. Sheila sat up in bed half asleep, half awake; she promised to call him soon after breakfast.

Soon after breakfast, Sheila called Dr. Sims.

At 5:45 AM, Megan waked on the couch, yawned, gave Gerald a broad smile, "Hi, sweetie, how was your day at the office?" she asked.

Gerald, more frustrated than ever, looked at her shaking his head, "Megan, what gives with this Melanie woman?"

Megan stood, tears welling in her eyes. "Why are you yelling at me?"

"Because here of late, you aren't the Megan I married." He moved toward the window, without looking at her. "Megan, are you impersonating someone?"

Megan got to her feet, rushed passed Gerald to the kitchen. "Why would you ask such a dumb question? Do you think I'm a crazy person?" she opened the refrigerator door. "Have you had dinner?"

"Dinner?" he stated calmly. "Hell, Megan it's 5:45 in the morning. An hour ago, I prepared a sandwich for your friend, Melanie." He kept his eyes directed on her face.

"Melanie? Gerald Price, I have no friend Melanie. Are you losing it? Honey, please? What's your point?"

Gerald took coffee from the canister; dropped it into the conical shaped filter; turned on the pot. Megan removed eggs from the refrigerator and placed them in a pan of water; turned on the stove's eye. She sat down near the end of the table, looking up like a frightened child, she said, "Gerald, do tell me more about this Melanie."

Gerald stole a cup of coffee before the pot had finished perking. Megan brought him toast and a boiled egg.

"Melanie? We can talk about her, but I'm more interested in Megan. It's time we see a psychiatrist." He nodded, "We're faced with something I can't explain."

Megan jumped to her feet, "Your insinuations I can't take, Gerald. You think something is wrong with my mind?"

Gerald hedged, realizing he'd pushed her to the limit. "Megan, you have a good mind, but you're personality is changing. The mind becomes ill like other parts of the body. You must see a doctor."

Gerald arrived at the office at 9:00 AM; loads of research material lying on his desk. He poured coffee, returned to his desk, picked up the receiver. Sheila's telephone number was busy. He waited a moment and dialed a second time. Sheila answered.

"Which Dr. Sims should I call, Mother?"

"Virgil, he'll give you good advice."

Hanging up, he decided to talk with Amanda first. She'd been a friend since childhood.

Amanda listened to Gerald, but realized Megan's problem was out of her medical field. She recommended Gerald stay put until she could talk with her fiancée in Chicago. "Gerald, Dr. Gray might know a specialist who treats this kind of illness." She promised to call Ted right away.

Hanging up, Gerald went to Jim Berry's office, Jim was on the telephone. The balding overweight lawyer, in his mid sixties, hung up the phone, turned in his chair, sensing Gerald's mood. "What's up, Gerald?"

Gerald hesitated a long moment. Berry at times could be crude, even overbearing, but Jim had a compassionate heart. "I'm not sure, Jim. I'm at my wits end." Gerald shook his head. "Megan's behavior is getting to me."

Jim got to his feel, moved around the desk to close the door. Jim listened to his problem; Gerald embarrassed to talk about his wife. "It started a couple weeks back. I went home to find Megan wasn't there. She came home past mid-night; a different person." Gerald rubbed his hands together. "What do you make of it?"

Jim walked to the window, looked down on the traffic below, thinking of his own wife who had died several years back. "A different person? What the hell is that suppose to mean? You're not making sense."

"Sorry, maybe I'm not...what I mean is...the woman was Megan, but she wasn't Megan. She called herself, Melanie." Jim's eyes narrowed; he focused on Gerald, something wasn't right. "Gerald, it's time you consult a professional. You're either sick or Meg is approaching a mental breakdown. Your wife came home, called herself by another name? It doesn't make sense. "

At day's end, Gerald rushed home, exhausted, the bed had not been made and breakfast dishes remained in the sink. He ran through the house calling her name; Megan wasn't there. He put on his coat, locked the front door and drove toward downtown. After an hour search of the west side, he spotted Megan's car at a night club. He pulled in beside it, quietly entered. There on the small stage was the love of his life, in a sheer dress he didn't know she owned. With her breast practically exposed, eyes half closed, she was singing *Blues in the Night.* His heart momentarily skipped a beat; Megan was actually singing; an act out of character. Megan was timid; she'd never perform before an audience. He located a table in the smoked filled room. His mind raced, his heart felt heavy, Megan was mentally sick. The waiter came. He ordered red wine, "Who is the singer?" Gerald asked, knowing the answer, seeking what the waiter knew about her.

The waiter chuckled, "Call's herself Melanie, just appeared out of nowhere; came in here this afternoon; asked for a job."

Gerald nodded, keeping an eye on Megan. "Is she from Birmingham?"

"Not sure. She's not on the payroll, yet. You sound interested," the waiter chuckled.

The band took a break; Gerald approached Megan, "It's time you come home with me."

"Come home with you?" Aren't you being forward, Gerald?" She laughed, taking a drag from a cigarette, "I've hated you forever."

"Megan, I'm your husband, you're not well. Come home with me."

"My name, Sir, is Melanie. Megan is not here." She looked at Gerald with contempt, "Now, will you please leave or shall I call the owner?"

Gerald's mind raced, frustration elevated his heart beat. No way could he leave her here. "Okay, Melanie, if Megan comes in tonight, will you give her a message?"

Melanie looked puzzled. "Give her a message?" she asked, mashing the cigarette in a tray. The band was now returning to the stage.

"Yes, tell her Gerald said, come home. He loves her."

Melanie got to her feet, returned to the stage. The band leader began to play *Love Letter's in the Sand*. Melanie began to sing. Gerald listened; he'd never heard Megan sing. She had a good voice. He checked his watch. It was time to get her out of this bar, his body ached for rest, but how could he get her to leave without creating a scene?

The song ended, Melanie left the stage for the lady's room. The band continued with its next number, Gerald kept an eye on the ladies room door. Megan appeared, looking into Gerald's eyes. She came rushing to his table, "What are we doing in this place?" she asked, a frightened look in her eyes.

Next morning Gerald returned to work with a queasy stomach. His frustrations were beginning to show. By the week's end, Megan actions had returned to normal with no sign or thought of Melanie. She settled into a normal housewife routine, but Gerald knew from what he had seen in the past, this behavior would not last, so his deep concern for her welfare mounted; Megan was sick. Melanie could appear any moment; Megan might not be home when he came in from work. He thought about his predicament; married to a lovely person who had a second personality entrapped within her body. Weeks went by without the least sign of Melanie. Maybe she would never return, but in his heart he had to face reality.

Thanksgiving Day, they joined other family members at the ranch for the holiday. Megan's mother, Dot Sutton, was invited. Nolan Garcia, now in his fifth year away from the ranch, came for dinner. Gerald noted for the first time that Nolen and his mother were growing apart. They were now two people sown together by matrimony, but tolerating each other;

preferring to go their own way. If their marriage were to last, Gerald recognized it was time for Nolen to get himself home to stay.

Before returning to Birmingham, Gerald and Megan dropped in on his grandparents at Rocky Mount. By day's end, the couple returned to Birmingham. Gerald's concern for Megan's mental health continued. Melanie could be lurking in the shadows of Megan's mind ready to show her undesired personality. He prayed she wouldn't return, but felt in his soul she would. Christmas was only a few weeks away. Late Saturday Gerald's heart sank; he recognized a personality change; Megan was acting differently. Moments later, Melanie, in a fit of anger began cursing Gerald's existence.

Chapter 4

December 1981....

With three days left before Christmas, Gerald hurried to finish his shopping before noon. He couldn't keep his mind focused or get excited over the season. His every thought was centered on Megan's condition. He locked his gifts he purchased in the car trunk and went upstairs to his office, shut the door and dialed Amanda Sims. His temples pounded, he took short deep breaths trying to relieve the tension. Amanda came on line. "Good morning, Gerald."

"Hi, she's shown up again. Did you talk to Dr. Gray?"

Amanda put him on hold, quickly moved to her office, shut the door; picked up the receiver. "Yes, Gerald, Ted recommends you find a local psychiatrist. I'd suggest you contact Dr. Claude Bennett at UAB. Claude and I were in medical school together. He's not a psychiatrist, but Claude knows every doctor in Birmingham. He'll give you sound advice."

Gerald spent an uneventful Christmas Eve at home, his thoughts centered on Megan's problems. At the moment, she was perfectly normal. Melanie left her during the night. Strange, but now Meg was happy again with no apparent problems. Gerald knew with no doubt Melanie was asleep lurking someplace in the shadows of Megan's mind, ready to spring forward like a vicious animal, taking over Megan's body at any moment. God, why couldn't he find a way he could help her through this crisis?

Christmas Day, he and Megan got up early, dressed and drove to the ranch to have Christmas dinner with Sheila and Nolen. The Garcia's, Nolen's parents, joined the event. It was a nice family gathering, but Gerald couldn't relax knowing Megan could change personalities as quick as she could speak. Before nightfall Gerald decided they should return to Birmingham. On the way home they sang Christmas carols, talked of soon starting a family. Happy go lucky Megan was filled with the spirit of Christmas, but Gerald's mind was fixed on what he had to do. He'd best follow Amanda's advice.

At 9:30 AM Tuesday, two days after Christmas, Gerald walked up the steps at UAB to the front desk and asked to speak with Dr. Claude Bennett. He was informed that Dr. Bennett would be out of the city for the remainder of December. "Could someone else help you?" the receptionist asked.

Gerald, not sure where to turn, decided it best to wait for Dr. Bennett to return. He left UAB, turned south on highway 280. An hour later he arrived at Amanda Sims' Clinic in the town of Sylacauga. He asked the receptionist if he could speak with Doctor Sims.

"Sir, she's in the lab. Could I give her your name?"

Gerald nodded, "Gerald Price."

Moments later, Amanda appeared, reached for his hand. "So you decided to come for a visit?"

"Yes, we must talk."

She turned to the receptionist, "We're going to the hospital break room for coffee. Hold any calls; I'll be back soon."

In the break room, Gerald looked at his watch; several people sat talking. Going through the line, Gerald purchased coffee, Amanda a coke. They moved to a table near the window.

"You're here to talk about Megan?" Amanda asked.

"Yes, Amanda." He frowned, pressure showing in his eyes, "She needs help...not the average shrink. Suppose you could talk with Ted again; I'm devastated for some advice."

His worried look bothered her. "Well, Dr. Hardgrove heads the Chicago Clinic. If you'd like, I'll ask him to set up an examination." Amanda paused, "Think Megan will be receptive to a Chicago visit for a few days?"

Gerald mulled the thought, "I'm not sure, Amanda." The agony in his eyes touched her. "I can't be away from the firm right now. Berry wouldn't approve."

They started to leave, Amanda suddenly stopped; her blond hair glistened in the morning sunlight. She thought of how much he looked like a frightened young boy. "Gerald, face facts, you may have to sacrifice for Megan's sake. Berry, be damned! Your wife is sick and Berry needs to know her condition." She kept her eyes fixed on him. "I'll get back to you after I've talked again with Ted."

They walked down the hospital corridor to the lobby. Amanda, stopped, looked toward the ceiling, a smile appearing on her face. "Gerald I may have a perfect solution. For a year now, Ted has been pushing me to visit his Chicago clinic." She frowned, looking toward the floor. "I'll have to take a couple weeks from my practice, but I need some time away." She nodded; Gerald could envision a plan developing in her mind. "I'll fly up in the Beechcraft and Megan can come along. I'll visit with Ted while Megan gets her examination."

"Come on, Amanda! That's too much to ask."

January 14 1982....

Monday morning, Gerald, along with Megan, took highway 280 south to Sylacauga, arriving around nine. At the airport, Amanda waited by the King Air Beechcraft. Arriving early, she had filed her flight plan then made her personal checks of the airplane.

Gerald quickly secured Megan's light suitcase in the rear seat then helped Megan into the co-pilot's seat; Amanda secured the doors, cranked the engines and taxied to the end of the runway. After a second check of her instruments, she revved the engines on the Blackhawk then sped down the runway, peeling the Beechcraft right toward Huntsville. She motioned for Megan to put on the headphones.

Amanda called Anniston Flight Service a second time. She would be flying VFR across country to Chicago's Midway Airport. Anniston's operator answered.

"Anniston, this is B4156. Could I have your latest weather report?"

"Weather in Anniston is currently cold and clear, below 12,000. Visibility is 7 miles. Surface winds 210 degrees at 6 knots."

"What's it like around the Chicago area, operator? Can you give me an extended report?"

"Forecasts along your route are winds aloft, all VFR with minimum ceiling 8000 broken at Nashville. A cold front is pushing southeast."

Amanda acknowledged. "What about the Chicago area?"

"Ma'am, visibility is forecast to deteriorate during the afternoon. Terminal forecast for Chicago follows: Midway from 1700 Z to 2000Z sky condition 4000 broken, 7000 overcast. Ma'am, suggest you update your weather briefing from Evansville. They'll have a better handle on the cold front for your destination."

Amanda took notes; thanked Anniston then placed the aircraft on cruise. Megan had dosed into a deep sleep.

Megan awaked; a slight turbulence tossed the Beechcraft downward and up again. Megan looked toward the earth below. They were flying over Huntsville. The Space Center, along a busy highway caught her eye. Amanda smiled then called Huntsville for permission to fly through the Space Center's airspace to give Megan a better look. She thought of Meagan's condition. A tour of the area might be an asset. After circling the Space Center, she turned toward Nashville.

"Megan, ever been to Chicago?"

"No, have you flown in there?"

"No, but don't worry. Midway isn't so busy."

Amanda was now over north Huntsville.

She turned to Megan, "Incidentally, we'll land soon for fuel and a pit stop."

An hour or so later, Amanda called the Nashville tower, requested landing instructions. The plane floated in on a north south runway. She taxied to a fueling station. Megan rushed to the restroom. They would take off again in fifteen minutes. Amanda remained with the aircraft until the refueling was completed. She rushed to the restroom then returned to the aircraft. Megan stood staring at her. Without conversation, they re-entered the aircraft. Amanda called for takeoff instructions. Moments later, the Beechcraft lifted off. Amanda veered north toward Louisville. With a few scattered clouds, they soaked in the beauty of the Cumberland Mountains. Amanda turned on the radio to a Louisville station. The soothing music soon put Megan to sleep. Looking to the west, clouds were gathering. Amanda decided to land in Louisville; she'd wait until the potential storm passed.

Unexpectedly, Megan waked shouting, creating a problem Amanda had not anticipated. Flinging her arms, Megan shouted, "You bitch, where the hell you taking me?"

Amanda, taken aback, kept her composure, her anger built, not at Megan, but at self for not anticipating this could happen. Melanie reached for the instrument panel; turned off the radio.

Amanda fought to control her emotions; looked at Megan. "Hello, Melanie. You are Melanie, aren't you?" Amanda asked.

Melanie shouted. "Why do you ask? Take me back to Birmingham, right now."

Amanda searched her mind, kept her focus; she was flying; couldn't lose sight of it, "Okay, Birmingham it is, first we must find a runway."

"No, turn around!" Melanie demanded, punching Amanda's shoulder. "Go back to Birmingham right now!"

Amanda nodded, "Okay, okay!"

Amanda searched for a place to land. To her right, she spotted a crop duster's field. "Melanie, we have to set down for a moment." She descended toward the landing zone. Melanie began punching her in the face, pounding her shoulders, grabbing for the controls. "You're not landing here!"

Amanda fought to bring the aircraft in to the landing field. She touched down, rolled to a halt. Breathing heavily, her heart pounding she lifted her voice. "Melanie you must allow me to fly the aircraft."

Melanie said nothing as she crawled from the cockpit. Before Amanda could release her seatbelt Melanie darted for a wooded area near the east end of the landing field. Out of no where, a farmer appeared in a pick-up truck. He stopped near the aircraft. "Ma'am, are you having trouble?"

Amanda frustrated, her face showing stress, "Sorry I had to land here. I'm a medical doctor transporting a mental patient who has escaped toward those woods." She pointed.

Along the bank of a narrow creek, Melanie disappeared. At a distance, an abandon mine shaft caught Melanie's eye; she entered. In darkness, she sank in a fetal position, cuddling her body close to the shaft wall.

Amanda, with the farmer close behind arrived at the creek bed. They looked at each other not knowing the direction Melanie had gone. The farmer shouted, "Ma'am, there's an abandoned mine shaft up there." He pointed, suggesting they take a look. Amanda led the way to the edge of the mountain searching for signs Melanie might have left. The mine shaft came in sight.

Amanda breathing deeply sighed with disgust, but collected her composure, "We must find her, she's sick."

"Ma'am, if she's here; we'll find her." The farmer pushed his way through tall weeds to enter the abandoned mine. He moved at a slow pace. Amanda followed. He cautioned, "Ma'am, watch your step; could be rattlers."

"Sir, what about a wild life officer?" Amanda asked.

The farmer nodded."One in town, but it'll take a while." He turned, a frown appeared. "We could call him in town."

"Sir, would you please call? I must stay here. She might decide to come out."

"Miss, it's getting dark. Aren't you afraid to be here alone?"

"I'll be all right. Please hurry." Amanda's voice carried urgency.

The farmer nodded, left in a hurry for home. Amanda cuddled near the entrance in scrub oaks; pulled her jacket tight. She sat there in silence until well after midnight; she drifted into a semi state of sleep.

Near daybreak she heard the rumble of a vehicle. Looking up she caught a glimpse of someone approaching; the farmer and wildlife service officer had arrived. After a brief introduction, without delay the officer, followed by the farmer entered the mine shaft. They traveled only a short distance, shining the light above, below, and to each side, looking for signs of Melanie, but also aware of rattlers. In a moment, Melanie's dress caught their attention. She was huddled near the mine wall; asleep. The officer touched her shoulder, "Ma'am, want you come with us?"

Melanie jumped to her feet screaming. The officer held her away from his body, her hands clawing at his face, her eyes sending fury. She continued to fight until exhaustion took charge of her body. The officer lifted her in his arms and carried her from the abandon mine; Amanda was waiting. He placed her on the ground; Amanda took her head in her lap."Officer, do you have access to an air ambulance?"Amanda asked.

"If it's not on call, Ma'am," Going to his jeep, he radioed. The county's air ambulance was available. The helicopter landed and paramedics took Megan aboard. Amanda crawled in by Megan's side.

At the hospital, they took Megan to the emergency room. While doctors examined her, Amanda remained in the hallway, found a telephone and placed a call to Gerald. He was appalled, but forced himself to face reality; Megan was sick.

When the phone went dead, he made a note. Her mother would want to know of the incident. He'd discuss with Dot Sutton what he should do next.

Amanda called her Sylacauga Clinic to check in. With no important messages, she relaxed. She'd be away for several more days.

They kept Megan in ICU for two days. Nurses removed the IV the third day. Amanda, exhausted from the experience, waited outside Megan's room. A nurse appeared, "Dr. Sims, she's calling for you."

Amanda cautiously approached Megan's bed, not knowing which personality would be present. "And who is here this morning?" Amanda asked, a curious smile on her face.

"You don't know me, Amanda?" Megan asked.

"Yes, honey, I know you well." She took her hand. "You ready to leave this place?"

By noon, Megan was released to Amanda's care. Before leaving the hospital, Amanda insisted Megan have a sedative. She would not risk another episode that could be fatal. She called a cab to return them to the parked

Beechcraft. After saying their goodbyes to the farmer and his wife, Amanda helped Megan fasten her seat belt. Once in the pilot's seat, she called Louisville flight service to file a flight plan. Moments later, she accelerated the engine; the plane launched forward picked up speed down the short runway. She pulled back the steering controls, the plane lifted off clearing tree tops on the north end of the field. Checking the fuel gage, she decided to re-fuel at Chicago's Midway Airport.

Megan slept in flight; Amanda turned on the news, but kept an eye on the weather. Before arriving at Midway, she noticed a sharp downward change in temperature. Moments later, she called Midway tower for landing instructions. Without delay, she set the aircraft down on the east west runway. Asking for instructions, she taxied to the fuel pumps. An attendant refueled the aircraft before securing it in a parking area.

Amanda led Megan inside to a phone booth. As she anticipated, Ted was in surgery. The receptionist would give him her message. She offered to send someone to pick them up; Amanda declined. They would catch a cab.

An hour later they arrived at the clinic. Megan was now acting normal. Melanie was gone for the moment, but Amanda cringed at the thought, knowing well Melanie could re-appear without warning.

Chapter 5

Third week January 1982....

By 3:40 PM with a nurse's assistance Amanda got Megan into a private room. Soon Dr. Jim Hardgrove stepped through the door, picked up Megan's chart. "Hello, Amanda, Dr. Gray's in surgery. He'll be along soon."

Amanda looked at the tall balding doctor remembering her father's admiration for his skills. Ted adored the man. Jim was known as the best in the business; had been for years.

Amanda nodded, a slight smile appearing. "Thanks. Dad sends his regards."

"How is the old coot?" Jim laughed.

"Fine, but he's working too hard."

Jim read Megan's chart with interest. He came to her bedside, began to check her pulse. He looked a second time at Amanda. "How's his health?"

She noted his deep voice resonate his words."Much

better since he quit cigarettes. He'll be retiring soon, so will Mother. Remember her?"

"Yes, you remind me of her."

"Thanks for the compliment."

Hardgrove stared into Megan's eyes. "I understand you've had an unpleasant experience."

Megan's quizzical look puzzled him.

"Are you referring to Amanda setting the aircraft down in that pasture?"

Hardgrove chuckled, "Well, that too, but how do you feel this morning?" he asked.

Megan paused, nodding, "Okay, but when do you plan to tell me why I'm here?"

The door opened and Dr. Theodore Gray stepped inside. A smile appeared when he saw Amanda, "Sorry I wasn't at the airport."

Amanda gripped his hand. "It's okay. We'll talk about the trip later."

Ted came to Jim's side, "How's she doing?" he asked. "Megan, "I'm Ted Gray."

Megan looked up, "I know. Amanda's told me about you."

Hardgrove ordered Megan a sedative; directed rest.

"What's up for tomorrow? Ted asked, looking at Jim.

"Bruce Holder is coming in."

"The psychiatrist?"

"Yep, you know Bruce; been around for years."

Jim, Ted and Amanda, left the room. A nurse entered, noting the sedative had taken effect, Megan was asleep.

At 8:oo PM, Ted and Amanda dropped by; Megan was still sleeping soundly.

"I have an extra bedroom." Ted offered.

She smiled, "That's enticing, but I'm at the Hilton."

"How about dinner?" he placed his arm around her shoulders. "It wouldn't be difficult for you to persuade me to take you to a local night club." He smiled.

"I'm not a good dancer." She looked into his eyes, shaking her head. "Ted, I didn't bring evening wear."

"Don't fret it." He smiled. "I know just the place."

"Oh? So that's why I can't reach you in the evenings?" She chided, a devilish smile appeared.

He nodded, looking at the ceiling, "Truth is, I've been there once. No female involved; you'll like the food."

"Ted, I'm tired. Could we turn in early?"

Ted drove south to the suburbs. The quaint place in a grove reminded her of home. The waitress seated them near the bandstand. They placed an order along with a glass of Chablis. Ted took her hand. "I'm pleased you've made it to Chicago." He pulled her to her feet. "Could I persuade you to join me here in Chicago?"

Scanning the audience, remembering a night they once spent in New Orleans, she looked into his eyes. "I'd love to be near you, but, Ted, I'm no city girl." They walked to the dance floor, "Dad will retire next year. Would you consider taking his practice?"

Ted pause, holding her in his arms. "I'm not a country doctor, Amanda. Doubt I'd be an effective there." He paused, cleared his throat, "I'll think about it." He took a deep breath; exhaled. "Dr. Sims may not agree."

She shook her head, "Don't be absurd, Dad has great respect for you."

At nine, the band took a break then returned. They began to play Ted's favorites *I'd do it all over again.* The thought of her being with him forever surfaced his mind; her slender body melted into his.

Near twelve midnight, she insisted they go. "I'm tired, Ted."

Ted drove her to the Hilton; kissed her good night. "We have much to do in the morning. Want to join me for breakfast?"

"Maybe; where?"

"At the clinic, I'll pick you up at seven."

Early next morning....

At 6:00 AM an LPN entered Megan's room. Melanie sat up in bed and demanded a package of cigarettes. The overweight nurse swallowed hard, not looking directly at her patient. She checked the chart a second time.

"Sorry Mrs. Price. No smoking in here."

"I'm not Mrs. Price, lady. You'd best bring me a damn cigarette!"

The commotion brought a nurse to Megan's room. She came quickly to Megan's bedside, attempted to console her, "Hold it, Ma'am. We'll consult with your doctor about the cigarettes."

Malanie frowned, her eyes like beads, the stare relentless. "Then get on with it. I want a cigarette now."

The nurse went to the hallway station, filled a syringe and returned to Megan's room. She motioned to the LPN. The larger woman pushed Melanie to the bed. The sedative relaxed her. She fell into a light sleep.

Later in the morning, Megan waked hungry. She pushed a button; the LPN came to her bedside, skeptical, "Yes, Mrs. Price?"

"When do you serve breakfast?" She asked. Her quiet voice was hardly audible.

Near eleven, Jim Hardgrove met Bruce Holder at the nurses' station. The head nurse led the way to Megan's room. Megan was sitting up reading.

Jim picked up her chart; came to her bedside. "Megan, this is Doctor Holder."

The small unattractive doctor's thick glasses set him apart. Her sullen look wasn't what Holder expected.

Megan's expression gave him a clue. Then she relaxed, her life depended on getting well, that is, if she were sick.

Chapter 6

January 25, 1982...

At 2:00 PM, a Trailways Bus pulled into the terminal at Sylacauga, Alabama's bus station. John, seated near the rear, waited to dismount. After retrieving his single piece of luggage, a worn army B-4 bag, he stepped from the terminal onto a sidewalk. He looked south, then north, not knowing which direction he should turn. He lowered his bag to the sidewalk; searched for a cigarette; lighted it. His head ached as he fumbled with thoughts; his mind questioning why he had come here in the first place. Faureta's thoughts sprang to his mind. He could hear his friend's counsel. "John, there's no reason to rush. Live one day at a time." He caught himself repeating Faureta's words aloud. Thank God no one was present to hear him.

The January north wind picked up scattering cinders from a nearby railroad over a wide area. The smell of the cinders, the railroad tracks, the sound of a truck crossing them, caused his body to shiver. He pulled his light jacket tight to his body. On Main Street north he entered a small café near the railroad tracks. It was an older brick structure that stood on a corner lot, a street ran north and south; a second small dirt street ran west of the building. John's heart warmed at the sight of the building. Was it the smell of food or did he recognize the place? What a foolish thought. How could he recall a place he'd never seen? The smell of hamburger meat cooking caught his attention. His heart pumped rapidly; had he been here before? Why did such thoughts pop into his head? Several people sat on stools at the counter. He chose a booth. A thin lady with graying hair and no make-up approached removing a pad from her apron. "Need a menu?" she quipped, looking into his eyes, popping chewing gum, raising her eyebrows.

"No, I'll take a cup of coffee, please."

The scars must have caught her attention. "Nothing to eat?" she asked.

Aware of her gaze, he nodded, "Yes, a cheeseburger." His heart warmed; the mirror above the counter, the appearance of the booths along the wall momentarily jolted his memory; the place seemed familiar, but why? Hamburger cooking smells the same in all restaurants, but this place....?

For no apparent reason, a young lady strolled into his mind, but quickly vanished. She seemed so young and pretty; God, if he could only recall. He took out a cigarette, asked if smoking was permitted.

"Yes, an ashtray is on the table."

He lighted the cigarette, looked at the clock on the wall. The Coca Cola advertisement caught his eye. He dunked the cigarette, pulled a second without thinking; did not light it. The waitress returned with his order. "More coffee?" she asked, picking up his empty cup.

John nodded, looking at himself in the mirror behind the counter, the scars obvious, but what the hell, they'd been there forever.

"Are you new in town?" she asked refilling his cup, setting it back on the table.

Not much for conversation, but realizing he shouldn't be rude, "Yes, I'm visiting someone." He paused sipping the coffee, again he caught a glimpse of his ugly scars the mirror. "Do you know a Price family who lives nearby? I was in the service with their son."

She frowned. "No, but Mom Callaway knows everybody in town."

Mom Calloway approached, "You asking about Don Price's family?"

The name Don he didn't register. "Maybe, I once knew Gerald, served with him in Korea. Ever hear of him?"

She nodded. "Yes, his mother comes in sometimes." She motioned toward Pop Calloway; he approached.

John shook Pop's hand, Mom looked at Pop, "You remember a Price kid, years ago?"

"Yep, back in the early 50's. Yeah, he and a Billingsley girl used to come here for lunch." Pop couldn't understand the boy's love for the army. "The boy hated school. What's your name again?"

John dunked a second half burned cigarette. "John Randall, Sir."

"You from round here?"

"I think I grew up in Columbus. Truth is; a war wound affected my memory."

Pop pointed north. "Six miles up that road is Morrisville. Gerald's family lives southeast of there; a place called Rocky Mount."

John finished his coffee; stepped to the curb and began to stroll north toward the high school. The cold wind had subsided; a light chilly wind felt good to his face. A voice called to him from across the street. He turned, a pick-up had stopped. The driver shouted. "You trying to find Gerald Price's family?"

John nodded, "I am."

The man opened his door, stepped to the street, "I'm Scott. Gerald's brother. Would you care to ride? I'm headed home."

John darted across the street and opened the passenger door. Scott had a beard, long hair and carried more weight than a man his age needed to carry. His rough boots and bibbed overalls added to his hill country appearance. The truck's cab was cluttered with beer cans and smelled of stale cigarette smoke. The truck cab smelled from Scotts sweat filled body.

"I don't know your family. You sure I'll be welcome?"

Scott pulled away from the curb, checked the review mirror, "Sure man. My parents will be glad to meet a friend of Gerald's."

Scott sped over a mountain, through a valley, past a cattle ranch. Just over a second mountain he wheeled right through a village. "This is Morrisville," he stated. "Dad works in that mill back there."

He turned left at the end of the village on to a dirt road. "This road will take us to Rocky Mount."

John looked across an open pastures at dormant grass, plots of brown and green, a few cattle lounging under an oak tree. His mind raced, his head ached. Faureta's counsel came to mind. Scott crossed a bridge, the vehicle bounced.

John listened with no interest to Scott described their neighbors along the way. He knew each by their first names.

"Where do you work, Scott?" John inquired attempting to make conversation.

Scott's eyes remained fixed on the dirt road ahead. "Sawmill at Rocky Mount. Make good money, but it's not regular; bad weather hurts us."

Severe pain again attacked John's temples; he reached for his brow. Sweat gleaned from his forward.

"You okay?" Scott asked.

John glanced out the window, back toward the driver. "Yeah, I'm fine."

Scott crossed a short concrete culvert then darted up a red hill. In a field sitting on a knoll a large frame house painted white came into focus. Scott began to slow. He stopped, opened a barbed wire gate, pulled the truck through and closed it. He thought the place familiar, relinquished the thought. Maybe Gerald had described it...

Scott halted the pick-up in the driveway; chickens scattered, feathers flying in every direction. Hanging baskets with winter plants hung on a worn back porch. At a distance, a small red barn stood inside a well defined fence. John's mind screamed to function. Had he been here before?

Nana Price, Scott's mother stepped to the back porch.

Scott shouted, "Mamma, this is John. He's a friend of Gerald's."

Stella, Scott's teenage sister came to the porch, eager to hear more. Nana welcomed their visitor explaining that Don, her husband, wouldn't be home until round six.

John was accustomed to a habit he had acquired years before. He made it a practice to display his better side. He kept his scars from view. Nana noticed, but she said kept quiet. She invited him to a front porch lined with four rocking chairs. They sat for a moment in silence; Nana's mind, filled with questions, eager to know what he knew of her son. "You served with Gerald in Korea?" her voice quivered, the question John expected.

John's answer was vague. He detected her expression. It made him question his knowledge of Gerald Price. Why had to come here? He must have known the man; he couldn't make up such a story.

She became more direct. "How did you meet Gerald?" she asked, her eyes revealing frustration.

"Ma'am, I think we joined an Army Unit in Korea on the same day."

Nana nodded, turning to look at Scott. "Scott, bring John's things to the guest bedroom. John, you will stay tonight, won't you?"

John, not sure why, but had no reason not to stay, removed his B-4 bag from Scott's pick-up and followed Scott to the guest bedroom.

Near 4:00 PM, Scott came to the porch. "John, I have to go in to Morrisville. Want to come along?"

The late evening traffic in downtown Morrisville was light. As Scott wheeled by a large store building,

John noticed the sound of band instruments. "Is that a band hall?"

Scott glanced, "Sure is; been here for years."

Scott crossed a railroad. Scott pulled to a stop in front of what appeared to be a grocery store. A sign over the front entrance confirmed Johns thought. "Vick Machen's General Store."

Scott darted inside, John followed; few customers were helping themselves. Scott went to the back and returned with a sack of feed. Vick, the store owner, kept an eye on the stranger. Something attracted Vick's attention.

Bubba Miller, a black man entered. The stranger caught Bubba's eye. The man's scarred face caught Bubba's attention. Memories of losing a leg in Korea came to his mind.

"Who is the man with Scott?" Vick asked.

Bubba shook his head, "Don't know, but he's been to war."

Loading his feed, Scott and John crawled into the pick-up to return. Swerving past the Company Store, Scott drove through the village pointing to houses filled with new families that had recently moved in.

A few minutes later, he turned up the driveway toward home. Don and Nana Price were sitting on the porch. A younger man stood talking to them.

"It's Gerald, Jr." Scott stated. "Wonder why he is here?"

Scott pulled the pick-up to a stop in the yard. Gerald stepped from the porch. Scott hurried to speak, "Gerald, this is John Randall, your father's army friend."

John extended his hand. Don Price got up from his chair. "Nana says you knew Gerald."

John nodded, words of doubt entering his mind, "Yes, but it's been a long time."

Don offered a rocker, Gerald remained close by. "Nana will have dinner soon. Where do you live?"

"Been in Tokyo since the war, Sir, but I think I grew up in Columbus."

John's mind struggled to recall. His mind screaming to remember what happened to Gerald. He stammered to explain with poor success. He couldn't recall Gerald's face or how Gerald died."

"Then maybe you didn't know Gerald at all." Don's stare pierced John's soul.

"I must have known him or why would I be here?" John asked, a frown appearing, "And, Sir, I have no recollection of my family in Columbus."

Don continued to stare; keeping his thoughts to himself.

Nana returned to the porch; Don offered her a chair. She asked John if he would stay for the week-end.

John nodded. "Sure I won't be a bother, Mrs. Price?"

Gerald sat on the steps, his eyes focused on John. "Mr. Randall, Grandfather has a point; maybe you didn't know my father." His remark cut deeply.

John nodded, giving Gerald a glance. "Could be, Gerald. I have no recollection except for his name. Maybe I've made a mistake coming here."

"An interesting thought, Sir. How did you find this place?" Gerald sat up to face the visitor.

John's eyes scanned the distant fields then settled on Gerald. He shook his head, a frown on his scared face. "Why? I wish I knew. I only know I left California, with no urge to go Georgia. For some reason, I wanted to find Gerald's parents. But I assure you, Gerald, I have no ulterior motive."

After dinner, Don went to the den, Stella disappeared to her bedroom. Nana cleaned the table and moved to the porch; asking John and Gerald to come along.

"Ma'am, I've told you all I recall about Gerald."

Nana touched his hand, "We understand. You've returned home; that's important. You must now find your own family. It's hard to lose a son in a war; we know."

Before mid-night, Gerald ended his visit. Driving back to his apartment in Birmingham he thought of John Randall. He seemed sincere; he could have known his father, but maybe the man was confused. Why would the man return to Morrisville if he had not known someone in the place? He decided to play the man's game, if he had a game. If he had an ulterior motive, sooner or later it would surface.

Silent Courage

Chapter 7

First week February 1982....

Monday morning, John took a shower, went to the kitchen. Nana poured his coffee, breakfast was waiting. Scott and Stella came to the kitchen.

After breakfast, John announced he would be leaving today. He asked Scott to take him to the bus station.

After breakfast, Don said his goodbyes then followed his routine; he headed for the mill; Nana cleaned the breakfast dishes; Stella walked to the road to catch the school bus. Before leaving, John went to the kitchen to say goodbye. Nana asked, "Will you come for another visit?"

"You're kind to ask, but I'm not sure."

"You're welcome here. Someday we hope to meet your family."

The bus pulled away from the Sylacauga Terminal for Columbus, Georgia. John took a window seat. Someone had left a copy of the Birmingham News. John checked the business page. Gerald Price, Jr. had been retained by an insurance company to handle a fraud case. Looking out the window he thought of Gerald. Gerald's father would have been proud of him. Why was he going to Columbus? An Army nurse, years ago, told him he was from the place; had family in Columbus.

Near mid-morning, John stepped from the bus. For no apparent reason, Columbus' main street was void of people. Suddenly, a sedan whizzed by. The color, the lettering...a military sedan; he'd seen many. Maybe he had been here in the military. He recalled the Infantry School was here. How did he know about Fort Benning? Where did he take training? A church bell chimed at a distance. The hymn...was familiar, but where was the church? Frustrated, he walked along the main street to a telephone booth. In the directory, he found the name Randall, but no John Randall. The court house would have a record of births in Columbus. If John Randall was born in Columbus, a record should be available. He flagged a cab.

Walking up the entrance steps, John caught a glimpse of a helicopter flying overhead. Should he visit the Fort? He could think of no ties with Benning. One thing was sure... he must establish a residence soon.

At the counter a young female asked, "Sir, may I help you?"

Without a thought, he stated. "Yes, I need of a copy of my birth certificate."

"Your name, Sir?"

"I'm John Randall. I'm a war vet and I've lost contact with my family. Could you help?" He asked.

She stared at John offering him a seat. She walked to a nearby filing cabinet. John's anxiety mounted, Faureta's advice came to his mind. What if she found his birth certificate? What would be his next move? Other people came in; a waiting line developed. The clerk called his name.

"Mr. Randall, birth records forty years ago were handled in such a fashion that we might never establish you were born here." She looked up. "Can you provide any information that might help us?"

John shook his head, "Ma'am, my Army Discharge shows I'm from Columbus."

The clerk suggested he inquire at Georgia's Bureau of Vital Statistics. John left the Probate Judge's Office for the Columbus Bus Station. On his way back to Birmingham, he decided he must hire an attorney. But first he had to establish a place of residence.

At 2:15 PM John's bus pulled into Birmingham terminal. He caught a cab to the Bankhead Hotel, checked in and searched the Telephone Directory for Gerald Price's home number. The phone rang...no answer. Gerald must still at the office; he'd call later.

He turned on the 6:00 PM news. The announcer gave

details of a new medical procedure open heart surgery developed at the University Hospital. Doctors opened the chest, removed veins from the legs to by-pass clogged arteries. Faureta once said someday a procedure would be developed to cover scars.

He went to the dining room. After dinner, he purchased a copy of the Birmingham News. At 8:oo PM, he called Gerald again. The phone rang twice...

Gerald's answered.

"Gerald. John Randall. Is this a good time to talk?"

"Yeah, how can I help?"

"I need a personal attorney. Would you be interested in representing me?" John asked.

Gerald hesitated then asked if they could meet at Joe's Restaurant tomorrow at 1:00 PM to discuss it.

The next day before noon, Gerald called Doctor Amanda Sims in Sylacauga. He wanted to inform her Megan was not on the mend. Amanda was out; he left a message. Slipping on a light jacket he left for Joe's.

Joe's restaurant was twenty minutes away. Hunger pains alerted him it was time for dinner. Moments later, he swerved into a parking space in Joe's parking lot; John was waiting. Loud music blasted. Seeing Gerald, John motioned to him.

Gerald took a seat. "What's on the menu? I'm starved." He stated.

"I'm having the dinner plate."

"So you've decided to live here in Birmingham?" Gerald asked.

"At least for the present." He paused. "I plan to rent a furnished apartment a month or so; have a suggestion?"

Gerald thought of a place owned by a client on highway 280 east of Birmingham. "You'll need a car, John. Birmingham is a big place, man."

"Tokyo wasn't a village, Gerald." He laughed. "A used car will do for now."

"Bobby Duke, south of here, sells good cars. We'll talk to Bobby. "

For the first time since leaving Japan, John felt he was alone. He tried reading, his mind wouldn't cooperate. What would Faureta say? "Patience man... patience." Faureta's lectures were lessons he must remember. He felt alone all right, but John was alone; no job and no chance of landing one. Brooding and self pity were not options. Should he buy a building, hang out a plaque? He'd talk to Gerald about it. Gerald would help him make important decisions. Why not? Gerald was now his attorney. Never again would he face depression alone. Faureta would say, "John, control your destiny."

Friday morning, second week March 1982....

John caught a cab to the south side; bought the 1977 Ford sedan Duke found at a sale. The same day, near highway 280, he located 400 acres of farm land for sale. Near the property's edge, he noted a Ford automobile with a real estate sign on the door. A female got out of the car, "I'm Jennifer with Birmingham Reality." She tossed her hair from her eyes.

Monday morning, he arranged to purchase the land. Gerald drove out Monday afternoon to take a look. The dwelling stood away from the highway in a clump of hardwood trees. John, with Gerald at his side, walked down the dirt drive to the dwelling. Evidence showed the place had been vacant for years. Gerald, shook his head, after a second look, "It'll cost you to renovate it."

"Yeah...I know."

Following Gerald's recommendations, John hired a builder. The old house was torn down; replaced with a small brick home at the same location. With his life savings dwindling John had to find a way to generate an income. Gerald helped to arrange a loan to build a small shopping center near the highway. In no time the rental spaces filled. Gerald kept a close eye in awe as thriving businesses sprang up in a few months. By September, John added additional buildings. By October's end, he opened his own therapist office. Before Christmas he hired a local housewife to assist him.

Tuesday morning, the last week of March 1982, John kept his appointment with Gerald. Arriving at 9:00 AM, he sat in the outer office waiting. Gerald appeared motioning John to his office. Gerald closed the door.

"John, I've worked on your project now for six months. Did you ever ride a roller coaster when you were a kid?" He kept his eyes on John. "It's like the roller coaster. I'm getting no place." Gerald tossed his pencil on his desk, took a deep breath, looked toward the ceiling. "I found a John Randall, Sr. living in Columbus. His son is missing in action."

Gerald handed John a photograph. "This is the missing man."

"Gerald? Hell, this man is black."

Gerald walked to the window, the traffic below moving along the busy street. "Yeah, I know. Where do we go from here?" Gerald returned to his desk. "Could it be you have the wrong identity?"

John frowned. "How would I know? I can't remember yesterday."

"Maybe John Randall, Jr. was killed in action and you're taking his place." Is that a possibility?"

John looked at his hands, no fingerprints. "I suppose anything is possible."

They decided for Gerald to try to find John's family two more months. He'd contact Department of the Army to verify his identity.

John got to feet. "Okay, I doubt the army would admit a mistake." He turned to leave, "How's Megan?"

"She's fine at the moment." Gerald sighed. "The other woman hasn't shown up in a while."

John chuckled, "You afraid to call her name?

"Hell, do I have to?"

"Think Megan might pay me an office visit?" John asked.

"You drumming up business or do you think you might help her? She's a private person you know."

John nodded, "But pills are band aids, your wife has a problem."

Gerald nodded, placing his arms across his chest, he shook his head. John was on target all right. Megan's condition worried him.

Chapter 8

Approaching winter of 1982...

In late fall a local farmer appeared in John's shopping center hauling a load of firewood. John made a purchase; directed him where to unload it. The November weather had moved in, wind scattering leaves raining from the oaks in John's yard. It had begun to turn cooler.

That night John built a fire, prepared supper to eat in the den. The telephone rang. Gerald sounded upbeat. Megan had agreed to be in John's office by nine.

At 10:00 PM, the fire turned to embers. John put up the night screen before going to his desk. On his yellow pad made notes. Megan supposedly is a dual personality. Could she be putting on an act? Why did Gerald choose a doctor in Chicago? Would the clinic in Chicago grant him access to Megan's records? Where did Megan grow up? Was she abused as a child? Hundreds of questions popped into his head; he needed answers. Gerald mentioned long periods of depression. She excelled in college; she should understand depression. He placed the pad on his desk. Was he capable of helping Megan?

Faureta helped him cope with an unsightly face, but Megan's condition was above his level of training. He'd never witnessed a person with a dual personality. He flicked on the television. The announcer was giving his nightly 10:00 PM newscast. He'd worry about Megan's problem tomorrow.

At 11:45 PM a car pulling into the driveway waked John. Who would be visiting this late at night? He got up, put on his robe. Through the blinds he recognized the vehicle. He turned on the porch light before opening the door; Gerald could hardly speak, "She's on the town again."

John invited him in, "When did she leave?"

"I'm not sure; Berry called a long meeting; I came in at eleven; the lights were out." Gerald's anxiety mounted. "This is her first time since Chicago."

John dressed while Gerald sat in the den waiting. They sped down the driveway toward highway 280. With his eyes fixed on the road, Gerald began, "I found her once at Town Bar on the northwest side."

"Should we try the place?"

Gerald paused. "I suppose; have to start some place."

On the northwest side they passed Birmingham Southern College going through a residential area. Gerald slowed looking for the old store building someone converted to a bar. A few cars including Megan's were in the parking lot.

Gerald checked his watch; 12:30 AM; loud music still rattling the walls. They entered, a stale smoke cloud hovered. Gerald surveyed the place, no Megan in sight. John waited nearby. A waiter located the manager.

Gerald gave him Megan's description, explaining the Ford near the building belonged to his wife. The manager recalled her being there earlier. "She often comes in and sings with his band."

"She came in today?" Gerald asked.

"Yes, ordered several drinks; left with a man." The manager paused. "Don't think the guy's from Birmingham." The manager signaled the bartender to announce the last round. He turned to Gerald, "My regulars say he's weird, but hell, most of them are weird."

"Weird? What kinda weird?"

The manager looked over the crowd. "What do you call a guy who enjoys dressing like a woman?"

"A cross dresser?"

The clock behind the bar showed 1:00 AM. John said nothing. It was Gerald's call.

The bartender again announced closing in thirty minutes. Gerald got to his feet; motioned John to leave.

A light wind had picked up, the southwest sky streaked with lightning flashes. "It's going to rain." John said. "Want to try another bar?"

Gerald shook his head. "It's useless. I'll go home. Maybe she'll come in soon."

"Shall I go with you?"

"Thanks for offering, but I'll manage."

"Have Megan come in tomorrow, okay?"

Gerald nodded, "I'll try."

On the way to John's home, Gerald talked without ceasing. Megan often got upset with her mother for no reason. Meg's mother seemed to thrive on creating friction. His incessant comments gave away family secrets.

"Who is... this Amanda?" John asked.

"Amanda Sims? She is a forensic scientist and pathologist in Sylacauga." He stated. "She's a family friend. Her father, Dr. Virgil Sims, is a well known physician in Talladega County."

"Suppose I could meet the lady?" John asked.

"Sure, just call her office."

Gerald dropped John off at home, day was breaking through the eastern horizon. Arriving home, Gerald pulled into the garage. In its special place sat Meg's vehicle. Tired from a night of worry he wrestled to control his anger. He quietly entered the kitchen then slipped into the bathroom. Without turning on the light, he took a leak, put on his pajamas, brushed his teeth and slipped into bed. Suddenly, Megan turned on her bedside lamp, "Where have you been, Gerald Price?" She asked.

Taken aback, he kept his composure. He wouldn't confront her at the moment. "I've been out with John for a drink; time slipped up on us." He rolled to his left side. "When did you get home?" He asked.

"I haven't been out all day."

Gerald, in need of sleep, yawned, "Megan, I have to be at the office by 10:00 AM."

Before leaving for work, he waked her. She sat up in bed; looked at him with sleep in her eyes.

"Want to meet me at Britney's for lunch?" He asked.

She agreed, but could be a few minutes late. She had things to do before she could leave home. Her blood shot eyes, the smell of cigarettes, tore at his heart. She walked with him to the door. He gave her a light kiss before backing from the driveway. Watching her re-enter the house, he wondered if she would be at Britney's.

Near 11:00 AM, Gerald's secretary buzzed, "Mr. Price, a Mr. Randall is here."

Why would John come in without an appointment? "Show him in, Sarah." Gerald directed.

John stepped inside and shut the door. His eyes showed concern, "Did you find her?"

The stress of no sleep showed in his eyes, "Yes...she

was home when I got there. What brings you here this time of morning?"

John asked for a cup of coffee. Sarah appeared with two cups; one for Gerald. John sipped, "My concern is you, my friend." He stared at Gerald. "You can't burn the candle at both ends."

"Damn, John, you're not my father. Cut the worrying crap, man. I'm fine."

His comment slammed at John's soul. He erased it; his mind slipped back to Japan.

Gerald noted John's deep thought; wondered what he was thinking.

John's mind drifted to what Faureta told him once of Doctor Hanaoki, The man developed the first anesthesia from plants. He was the first to remove a cancerous breast from a woman. God, old Faureta held Hanaoki in such high esteem. John's mind fast forwarded to the University of Tokyo. He once dreamed of becoming a medical doctor. Faureta encouraged him, but the war scars...?

John, then felt guilt; he was burning Gerald's valuable time. He got to his feet. "I'll talk with you tomorrow."

"Are you, okay, John?"

"Yes, but I don't suppose that's your concern. Are you acting like a son?"

John shook his head a smile appearing, "Thanks, my friend. You have a good day."

Near lunch time, the telephone rang a second time, John picked up the receiver. Still in his farm work clothes; the morning had been busy; a day when his secretary must take leave. The voice was pleasant. "Good morning, Mr. Randall, Megan Price. Gerald asked me to give you a call."

Not expecting Meg to call so soon, he took a deep breath, "Yes, Mrs. Price. You feeling well today?"

Megan nodded, "Yes, Sir, Gerald said for me to make an appointment. Are you a medical doctor?"

John laughed, "No, Megan. I'm a therapist. Gerald tells me you have been having problems." He paused.

Megan switched the telephone to her other ear; picked up the diet coke on the end table. "I'm not sure what Gerald meant by problems." She paused, "But to satisfy his mind...could I come in around 2:00 PM today?" she asked.

John had painters working at the barn. "Yes, I'll be here."

The phone went dead; John rushed to prepare to meet Meg.

Silent Courage

Chapter 9

November 1982...

Britney's was crowded at noontime. They ordered, ate with little conversation then departed going their separate ways. Megan hurried northeast to John's office, arriving near 1:15 PM. The small shopping center was crowded. She located a parking space. John's office had such at quaint look. She waited for a receptionist, no one came. Suddenly, John appeared. The slim well built man appeared to be in his mid fifties. Dressed in slacks with an opened collar, his graying hair gave him a fatherly look. John, apologetically, told her of his scarred face. "I'm alone today." He stated, "My receptionist's son is in a school play." He offered Megan a chair. "It's hectic without help."

Megan stared, "Why am I here?"

"You may have a problem we need to discuss." He paused looking into her eyes. "I know of your Chicago treatments."

Megan, squirmed, a bit embarrassed. "What other family secrets has Gerald told you?"

"Don't be offended. Gerald is concerned about you."

Her eyes focused. "I've seen the best psychiatrist in all of Chicago. Why should I come to you for treatment?"

John was impressed. "You've asked a good question, Megan."

John told her of his experience during the war. The scars were the result of a flame thrower. He had spent hours in therapy to overcome depression. The therapy had saved his life. He learned the Japanese language and attended therapy training at Tokyo's University.

"But Gerald says you had a family in the States?" She interrupted.

"Yes, Megan." He moved to the window, frustration filling his chest. "Have you looked at my face?" He asked, turning the scars toward her.

Megan nodded, "Yes, but those scars are no excuse for not coming home." She frowned, "I can't believe you allowed scars to keep you away from your family!"

John moved back to his desk, "I suffered from depression. Have you ever been so depressed that you wished you were dead? I didn't care to return. I felt people would look at me as a freak."

Megan shook her head, "Poor excuse. And you're a trained therapist?"

Yes, he was a trained therapist, but she made him wonder. However, he had succeeded in capturing her attention. "But I can't recapture time, Megan."

He began to tell her about his friend Faureta. Faureta came from Sendai a large city north of Tokyo. Anoka Faureta trained at Tokyo's University under Japan's best therapists. "I was one of Faureta's first patients." John explained that he lived in a flat in downtown Tokyo, found the Japanese to be friendly so he adapted their culture and accepted their ways. He told her of the many hours he spent burying himself in his school work, praying to overcome his conditions. Busy work kept him from losing his mental faculties. After years of study he earned a degree. Japanese doctors did plastic surgery on his face. But Dr. Faureta, the psychoanalyst, pulled him from the depths of despair. He told her of a time when he had planned to commit suicide, but Faureta brought him back to reality. "Now, to answer your question...why did I decide to return?" A smile appeared on his face. "I suppose every human being has a desire to be loved. It's difficult to explain. I think of Maslow's Hierarchy of Needs. We all have needs." He paused, looking into her eyes. "Do you understand?" He asked.

Megan, looking perplexed, "I want Gerald's love, but I'm not interested in that Maslow stuff."

John laughed at her basic honesty, "Okay, sorry I mentioned it. Tell me about yourself."

"I grew up in Montgomery, attended Birmingham Southern College and after graduation, Gerald and I got married and a few months later, Gerald and Mother say I got sick."

"I'm told you have two personalities?"

"Maybe at one time, but no longer; that's behind me." Megan stated. "I don't care to discuss it."

John got to his feet, tugged at the back of his neck, "If that second personality no longer exists, why is it difficult to tell me about it?"

Megan's eyes narrowed, raising her voice, "Just skip it, John."

Scrambling to his feet, John picked up his coat. "Okay, I will." He paused, glancing at the floor. "I'm going out to the farm to check on my workman. Would you like to come along? I'd love your opinion on something I'm planning to do..."

Traffic on 280 was slow, but he arrived, opened the door for Megan. Two yellow labs welcomed them. "Careful, Megan, they'll jump up on you."

She laughed. Something about John Randall she couldn't put her finger on. Was it his voice or mannerism? He led the way to the barn. Several black men stood on scaffolds. The man with the spray gun kept moving; paint flowing; covering the rustic wood. John marveled at how a single coat could change the appearance.

Walking back toward the house, John stopped in front of a small row of azaleas. He picked off several dry leaves. "Megan, I need someone to advise me on how to improve this yard." He walked to the opposite side picking twigs and dead leaves. "Are you be interested in such a job?"

She frowned. She once wanted to study landscaping. "You would consider me? I'm not trained in that field, but I think I'd like that kind of work. Could I have time to discuss it with Gerald?"

"Sure, no rush."

"If I accept, I'd like to visit a couple of nurseries."

"An excellent idea, Meg."

John smiled at the thought. It would be great therapy; the work could only help.

She nodded, "Can I have someone from a nursery pay us a visit before we decide what to plant?"

"Sure, a couple if you'd like."

Tuesday morning Megan got out of bed dressed quickly and prepared Gerald's breakfast. Gerald came to the kitchen not believing Megan was singing while she watched the bacon fry. "Good morning." She smiled when Gerald entered." It's going to be a good day. The weatherman predicts great weather." She broke eggs into a cup, mixed a bit of cheddar.

Gerald asked, "Why are you so happy?"

She carried his breakfast to the table, "Coffee?" She asked. "I'm meeting a horticulturist from Green Thumb at John's place at nine. Gerald, I'm so excited about John asking me to oversee the work in his yard."

Her attitude thrilled him. She brought him a second

cup. "John believes in me. I'm actually going to landscape his yard. Can you believe it?"

"But, you've never landscaped a yard before," he stated.

"No, but I've wanted to try."

Gerald sipped his coffee, "Do you find John amazing?" he asked.

She mulled his question. "Not sure amazing is the right word." She took a seat next to him. "He's fascinating, intriguing, interesting. Yes, that's the quality I like best; interesting. John Randall is interesting."

Gerald smiled, "I have to agree he has charisma. Do you want to do this...landscaping?"

"Yes, unless you object."

"No objection, Megan, it's your call, but you'd better enjoy digging in the soil."

She moved toward him, placed her arms around his shoulders, "Gerald, this could help me; that is, if I've been ill."

He smelled the aroma of her perfume, touched her hands gently and kissed them. "Okay, if John wants you to landscape, he has a reason."

Gerald put on his coat. "When do you plan to begin?"

"Today, soon as I can.

Megan explained she planned to go to the farm to

meet two people from a nursery. He kissed her, picked up his briefcase. "Have fun, see you tonight?"

John watched from the porch; Megan's white Chevrolet sped up the driveway. This could be the beginning of a good relationship with Megan Price, only time would tell. She came to a halt, crawled from the car, a yellow pad in her hand. She ran up the steps, "John it's a good day to play in the back yard," she said. "I have two people coming to give us ideas."

John smiled, "Would you like a cup of coffee?"

She stepped to the kitchen table. The coffee was steaming. She took a sip, "John, would you consider a small fountain this side of the azaleas?"

"Only if you'll keep its size within reason."

"I've selected an inexpensive one."

John laughed, "That's good to know." John refilled his cup, "Let's go to the porch."

"Okay... but only until those men arrive."

John took a seat in his rocker; she took one nearby. "Megan, tell me about Melanie."

"Do we have to talk about her today?" she asked. "I pray she's gone forever."

John didn't press her. Before noon the two men arrived. The older held a plan for the fountain's location; the other presented Megan with a potential plan for shrubs and bedding plants. By noontime, they began the groundwork. With minor changes, John accepted her plan. It had been a long morning. John and Megan agreed to a needed rest.

After lunch, Megan went to the porch. Megan shocked John, "Okay, now we can talk about my sister."

Megan told of her first encounter with Melanie at the Chicago clinic. Dr. Holder, a Chicago psychiatrist, diagnosed Megan's condition.

She told him of Gerald finding her in a bar dressed like a hooker. It was Melanie, not her. She only wanted to go home.

Melanie appeared to Megan the first night at the Chicago clinic. The two had a sisterly talk. Megan told John of how she had accepted Melanie as a friend.

Dr. Bruce Holder diagnosed her problem almost immediately. A few minutes into Megan's first counseling session, Melanie surfaced. Holder diagnosed Dissociative Identity Disorder. Holder's therapy assured her Melanie was no longer present. Megan was informed by Holder that she could live a normal life.

John walked to the back porch; Megan followed. "How about us taking a horseback ride this afternoon?" he asked.

The idea caused her to smile. John took a seat on the steps; inviting her to sit also. "I'm not a horse person."

"Okay, but I can teach you." He looked up to see geese flying south. "Want to tell me more about Melanie?" He asked.

"No, I haven't seen her since Chicago. She's gone for good."

"No, Megan. Melanie returned a couple of weeks ago. Gerald should have told you."

John saddled two horses; helped her mount the gentle one. Leaves had begun to fall covering the trail leading toward the back pasture. John mused at her interest in simple things; she watched leaves float to the ground. At a distance, near John's fence line, they approached an old fenced cemetery. Years of standing in weather had left tombs stained. "Who is buried here, John?"

John dismounted, assisted her to the ground. "I'm not sure, Meg. This is my first visit back here."

"John Randall? You purchased this property without looking at every foot of it?" She laughed.

The two walked to the cemetery. The first tomb was engraved, *Henry W. Strickland. Born 1824, Died 1876.*

"I assume we're in a Civil War cemetery." John stated, folding his arms to his chest.

Megan moved among the graves to find those buried here were near the same age.

"I'd like to find out more about this place."

John laughed, "Why waste your time on this, Megan?"

She frowned, "You're not interested? It's a part of our heritage."

They sat on the trunk of an uprooted tree. John seized the moment. "Megan, Melanie is still in your subconscious." He paused, selecting words. "When she comes to you again refuse to accept her friendship."

"I don't think she'll return, but, she's nice, John."

"Nice? No, she isn't. She's playing a game, Megan. She wants your whole world."

Megan nodded, looking at the sky above; appreciating his concern.

She walked toward her horse, "I'll keep that in mind." She smiled, "Would you please help me up?"

He moved to her side, coupled his hands, making a step.

At the barn, John removed the saddles, turned the animals loose into the corral. They walked to the porch. John brought her a drink of water. "Can we meet again tomorrow?" he asked.

"I suppose, after my meeting with the guys about bedding plants." She got to her feet, "Could I use your telephone?"

"It's in the hallway," he suggested, gazing at his new fountain, proud of its appearance.

Megan picked up the receiver, suddenly feeling faint. She cringed at the thought. Melanie replaced the telephone. Melanie went to the kitchen. Seconds later, she plopped into a rocker beside John, lifting a leg over the chair's arm. "Have you lived out here long?" she asked.

John cleared his throat, surprised. "So you've come for a visit?" He shrugged, keeping his eyes on the fountain.

She laughed. "You know about me?"

"Oh, yes, I'm aware of you, Melanie."

Melanie laughed, "Why do you like Megan so much?"

John selected words, "Megan is a friend's wife. Why do you ask?"

"You have poor taste, Mister."

Her words filled with sarcasm, John ignored it, "I thought Megan was your friend."

She shrugged, "Nope, she isn't. Do you have a drink in the house?"

"I have a bottle of wine."

"I'd prefer a martini."

John went to the kitchen; returned with a glass of wine.

Handing it to her, he asked, "How long have you known Megan?"

"Why are you so interested in that bitch?"

He gave no response. "Megan thinks you're her friend."

John observed her pupils. "Let's talk about you, Melanie. I'd like to know you."

"Then, let's go to a bar. I want a martini."

"Can we wait a while?" He removed a gold watch from his pocket. "Have you seen this watch Megan gave me?" he asked.

"I'm not interested in your watch, Mister."

John pressed her to look, the watch dangled, her eyes closed. She succumbed to his voice. What questions would Faureta ask? Not sure this type of treatment was in Megan's best interest, he backed away. He wasn't a psychiatrist. Megan needed to return to Chicago. But he could talk with Melanie.

"Melanie, could I speak with Megan?" John asked.

Melanie frowned "Megan's not here." She shook her head. John sensed resentment. She lashed out, "Megan can't control me anymore." She began to cry, "Megan isn't fair. She lies."

"Why do you claim her for a friend?" he countered.

A frown appeared. "She's not my friend. Megan's a bitch." She shouted tossing her head back. "She thinks we're friends."

"Where is Megan at the moment, Melanie?"

She laughed, another frown appeared. "She's inside. I plan to keep her there."

John took note; Megan must be the stronger of the two. Melanie could only surface when Megan allowed it. John snapped his fingers, Megan returned. She gazed; then smiled. "Hi, John, it was a great nap. What time is it?" Megan asked.

"Who am I talking to?"

She frowned, "John, are you all right?"

He laughed, "Yes, Meg. I'm fine, but we have much work to do."

She got up from the chair, "I know...it's going to take a while, but the yard is coming along fine. Could we get it featured in a magazine?" she asked.

He nodded, looking into her eyes, "We'll talk with Gerald about it."

For the remainder of the year, John kept Megan busy with jobs that required her to dig in the soil, plan, and develop new ideas. She had little time to think of her ailment.

Chapter 10

April 1983...

Thunder shook the building. The telephone rang in Amanda's office.

The receptionist's picked up the receiver.

"Doctor Sims, Mr. Price is on the phone."

"Will you be in your office tomorrow?" Gerald asked; an urgency in his voice.

"Yes, until 3:00 PM. Is Meg all right?"

"Yes, but we need to talk."

"Come at noon. We'll have lunch."

Amanda stared at the telephone. There had to be a way to rid Megan of Melanie. She had to discuss it with Ted.

John dreaded the two hour drive from Birmingham to Columbus, but the trip was necessary. Gerald's detective located a Randall family on the southwest side of Columbus. At 10:00 AM highway 280 traffic was almost nonexistent. He observed a slight traffic increase at Childersburg and a second at Sylacauga. An hour later, he arrived in Columbus.

He parked along the curb, walked up a flight of steps at the courthouse. A familiar pain, one that troubled him frequently, shot through his brain; pain that brought on anxiety. For an instant, he thought of walking away, but Dr. Faureta's counsel intervened. John, never give up; he had no choice but to stay.

At a counter in the courthouse, he went to a clerk. "I'm trying to locate a John Randall. Could you help me?"

"Were you here before?"

"Yes, couple of months ago."

"We couldn't find your birth certificate then. Sir, nothing has changed.

We have a John Randall, Sr., but he is a black man who lives on the southwest side."

John jotted Randall's address. He left the courthouse. Frustrated, he decided to drive to the southwest side of town. A light breeze blew in off the Chattahoochee. The river ran along the west side of the street. The west section was cluttered with small well kept frame houses.

John pulled into the Randall's dirt driveway near 11:00 AM. An elderly black man and woman sat on the front porch of the two room dwelling. The beagle hounds at the man's feet announced a visitor. Neither the man nor woman moved; only stared.

John asked. "Are you Mr. Randall?"

They looked at each other; the man nodded. "I'm John Randall."

John moved closer to the steps, the dogs calmed. "I'm John Randall, Jr. and I'm looking for my parents."

The man chuckled. "Well, ain't you white?"

John nodded. "Yes, I'm white, but may I ask you few questions?"

The man looked puzzled. "What you want to know?" he asked.

"Did you your son to serve in Korea?"

The woman quickly answered. "Yes, he's been missing since the war."

"Was he John Jr.?"

"Yes, he's missing; not dead."

"Was your son in the army?"

The man frowned, nodding his head. "John is still in the army."

John moved to the porch's edge to sit down. "In the infantry, I suppose?"

They looked at each other. "Yes."

John got to his feet; looked toward the river and turned to leave. "I thank you for your time."

John, convinced he had no family in Columbus asked himself what Dr. Faureta would do in his situation? Had the army blundered? The identification tags found by his side belonged to John Randall, Jr. What happened to those tags? They were not returned to him. He only had Faureta's word. Maybe Gerald could give him some advice. Should he forget family and return to Japan?

John walked up the steps from his back yard near noon. On the back porch, he took time to admire his new fountain. The bedding plants added color.

He turned to Megan; taking a well deserved break on the porch. "Meg, I love the yard. It is more than I expected." John wiped his brow, looked into her eyes, "I'm hungry. Are you ready for lunch? I'll stick a pizza in the oven."

"Sounds delicious," She stepped to the edge of the porch. "Could I use your telephone?" she asked.

"Sure." John pointed.

In the living room, she picked up the receiver...

Gerald's secretary answered. "Megan's on the line, Mr. Price."

"Where are you?" He asked.

She laughed, "This is not Melanie, dear."

"That's not funny, Megan." He paused. "I'm worried sick about you. What is going on? Where are you?"

"John's fountain is complete and the yard is developing as planned."

"What is so unusual about that? I expected it, Megan."

"Don't be so curt, Gerald. I won't you to see it."

"Is John pleased? That's what matters."

"Yes, but after work, you run by John's and take a look. When you get home, I'll have dinner waiting."

Has a simple success changed her attitude? "Where are you having lunch?" he asked.

"John's heating a pizza. Want to join us?"

"Meg, I'm up to my ass in research." He tossed his pencil on his desk. "Tell John I'll see him about 5:30."

After pizza and coke, Megan slipped to the back porch to nap in John's hammock. John came to his rocker. He pondered Megan's illness. How could a vibrant healthy female have such a problem? Dissociative Identity Disorder? Never in his wildest dreams did he expect to encounter such a case. Her breathing was like a child with no worries. Gerald loved her so much, but he was another worry. Why had he allowed Gerald to become so special? His helping Megan meant much to Gerald. Faureta once said everyone needs to be surrounded by other human beings. Did he need to locate his family? Maybe, but Gerald and Megan were his family at the moment. Faureta, the old bastard should be here. Should he call Faureta? Maybe not; even Faureta would need time to study Megan's case. John rocked, lecturing himself. With great mental health facilities under his nose, surely they could find a cure for Megan. He thought of her options. She could go to Japan for a visit with Faureta, but Gerald couldn't take time from the office. If Gerald could take off from work, traveling to Japan would cost a chunk. Maybe Faureta could come here, but Faureta was a sick old man; no way would be come to America. Another option would be to continue work on Megan's self esteem, keep Melanie away. Megan would have to stay busy with no time for depression. Gerald would need to cooperate. Bruce Holder's assessment of Megan's illness wasn't questionable. So, a psychiatrist must be called in. He once studied about Multiple Personality Disorder but, that was year's ago. Was it possible for two personalities to occupy one body? Holder said Megan had less than one well adjusted personality. What would Fauret say?

Megan turned to her other side; continued her uninterrupted sleep. John eased from his chair; entered the kitchen for a drink of water. Suddenly, the telephone rang. Amanda Sims wanted to speak with Megan.

At 6:30 PM, Gerald's car pulled into his driveway. Megan met him at the door. "Did you go by John's" she asked.

He closed the door, kissed her. "Yes, the fountain is nice." He hung his coat in the closet. "John says Amanda called..."

"Oh yes, and guess what! She's buying her father's airplane."

Gerald went to the refrigerator to open a beer, "So Dr. Sims is giving up flying?"

She continued to place dinner on the table. "Amanda didn't say." She walked to the west window to close the blinds. "Gerald, did your mother tell you Ben is going into the army?"

"No, where did you get that information?"

"Amanda told me today. He's going to an Officer Basic Course."

"That's interesting." Gerald nodded, "When does he leave?"

"The first week in November, I believe." She motioned him to the dining room. "Let's eat while it hot."

After dinner, Gerald called his mother. She wasn't pleased that Ben was leaving for the army. She also expressed displeasure at being left at home alone; Nolen spent most of his time working with the ABI on a case.

"How much longer will he be gone?"

"Not sure, maybe a couple of months, but I'm tired of it."

"Mom, try not to worry. Ben will be fine. Where will he go for training?"

"Fort Hood, Texas."

"Fort Hood? That's interesting. Didn't you say Dad trained there?"

Gerald hung up; turned on the six o'clock news, but he couldn't help but think of his mother. It was time for Nolen to get his butt home.

Moments later Megan answered the phone, "It's for you."

Chapter 11

June 1983....

John Randall stepped from the elevator at 9:30 AM and entered Gerald's main office. He had an appointment in five minutes.

In Gerald's private office he reported the results of the Columbus visit. John didn't find a birth certificate in Columbus. However, he found that a black man with that name had once lived there. The black John Randall was an infantry soldier missing since the war.

Gerald listened. When John finished his report, he looked up from the writing pad, "John, I have an old classmate who is head of Georgia's Bureau of Vital Statistics. I'll touch base with him tomorrow. If you were born in Georgia there should be a record of your birth."

"Tomorrow?"

"Yes. Count on it."

John nodded, accepting that Gerald couldn't call today. He changed the subject, taking Gerald by surprise,

"Incidentally, can Megan come in early tomorrow and feed the horses? I have an early appointment."

Gerald laughed, "Are you out of your mind? Megan feed horses?"

"Yeah, she's good with the horses." John paused. "And it might surprise you to know, I'm in the market for a few Black Angus. Have any ideas?"

Gerald chuckled, "Don't tell me you're joining the Cattlemen's Association. You'll regret buying those damn things."

"No, I'll enjoy them, any suggestions?"

"Will you be free Saturday? My mother raises Black Angus."

"Saturday sounds Okay, Let's take a look."

Wednesday morning, John waked with rain striking the metal roof. He got up, dressed quickly, prepared breakfast. Before daybreak, he left for the office. His first appointment arrived before 8:00 AM. It was a busy morning, meeting with several different patients. Megan's illness kept creeping into his mind. He thought of Dr. Holder's successful counseling sessions. Holder was a qualified psychiatrist.

A physical therapist couldn't measure up in Meg's case. No, Megan should pay Holder a second visit. Searching his mind, he accepted his inadequacies to deal with Megan's condition. Faureta hammered the fact that a therapist should not take on a job of a trained Psychiatrist. John dialed long distance. Amanda Sims' receptionist answered...

John glanced at his desk calendar. It was already late June. The year was flying by.

"Could I speak with Dr. Sims?" he asked.

"She's in the lab. Could I take a message?"

"Yes, I'd like to make an appointment with the doctor."

"Dr. Sims doesn't see patients anymore. She's into forensic work."

"I understand, ma'am, but I need to talk with her about a mutual friend."

"Please hold."

John waited. Faureta's counsel came to mind. *People will try your patience.* Moments later, Amanda breathed into the telephone. "This is Dr. Sims"

"Dr. Sims, I'm John Randall, a friend of Gerald and Megan Price. Do you have a moment?"

"Are you calling about Megan?"

"I am...will you be in tomorrow morning?"

The receptionist reminded her of a Wednesday appointment in Montgomery.

"Could you be here around eleven? We can talk over lunch."

The trip to Sylacauga seemed short. John turned on the morning news. Reagan's proposed tax cut had a democratic congress in a fury. The parking lot at Amanda's clinic was practically empty. He checked his watch; five minutes early. Something about Sylacauga stimulated his mind. Why did the place seem so familiar? Gerald Price's family came to mind. He hadn't kept his promise to visit. He locked the car door, bounded up a flight of steps. Dr. Sims was waiting.

At Amanda's suggestion, they walked across the street to have lunch at Sylacauga's hospital cafeteria. She led the way through the line. John noted she ordered a light lunch. They located an empty table near the north east corner. John kept his scarred side turned from her direction. Soon their conversation turned to Megan.

John came to the point. "I'm not sure my counseling is helping Megan. She is responding, but her progress is slow. And her antagonist Melanie has re-occurred of late. I've kept Megan doing projects; digging in the soil on my mini farm..."

Amanda nodded, "That's good therapy. Megan is sick, no doubt."

Though he tried to keep the scars hidden, he failed; they were distracting. "How can I help Megan?" she asked.

"Dual personality syndrome is a tough job for a psychiatrist and far beyond my pay grade. Megan has mentioned Dr. Holder. She has great respect for him. I think she needs additional counseling."

Amanda frowned. "I'm sure it can be arranged." She hesitated, her attention drawn to John's face.

"I'll talk with Dr. Holder." She made a note. "Will Gerald agree to her returning to Chicago?"

"We haven't discussed it, but I don't think he'll object."

Amanda couldn't leave without bringing up John's face. She looked into his eyes. "Have you thought of plastic surgery?" Her sincere look caught his attention.

Taken aback at her boldness, John cleared his throat. "Yes, I've had several operations. I apologize for my unsightly appearance..."

"No apology necessary. Things have changed in the past few years. Plastic surgeons today are performing miracles. Give yourself a chance to live again."

They walked to her office. John told her goodbye. "It's been a pleasure, Mr. Randall."

"I'm John, remember?" his laugh was contagious.

"Yes, John. I hope to see you soon. Will you consider my advice?"

John frowned, "You think my face can be repaired?"

"Yes, if we select the right plastic surgeon."

John turned north toward Birmingham. Over the mountain, he passed by the remains of a night club. The doors long since closed; the sign near the entrance read *The Cocoanut Grove*. John wondered if Gerald Price, Sr. ever visited the place before the war. Going over Red Mountain, down through the valley, the returned trip seemed much shorter. Suddenly, his thoughts were consumed with Amanda's recommendation. Why would this young forensic doctor who knew so little about him be interested in helping him? It didn't make sense. If she could find a plastic surgeon, he'd undergo another operation. At the moment Megan's health was more important. For Gerald's sake, Megan had to get well. He'd call Gerald tonight.

At 6:30 AM Saturday morning John's telephone rang. He reached for the receiver wondering who would call so early.

"John, Gerald...we'll have breakfast on the road."

John, half awake, half asleep, sat up on the side of the bed, "Where are we going?"

Gerald laughed. "It's Saturday morning. Remember you wanted a few brood cows?"

"Sorry, Gerald, I'd forgotten." John bounded from bed, dressed quickly, and made a pot of coffee. Gerald would pick him up in 30 minutes. John downed a cup before going to feed the animals. When he returned Gerald was on the front porch.

The trip down 280 to Childersburg took less than forty minutes. Gerald darted into a spot at Ryan's Café. They ordered breakfast. John, excited about his conversation with Amanda began to talk about Dr. Holder. Megan must receive additional counseling.

"I'm not sure this is a good time." Gerald loaded his coffee with cream and sugar. "You see, Megan..." John read his displeasure. "Well, I'm not sure this...."

The waitress appeared with food. She closed the blind to keep out the sun. John continued. "Why would Megan object?"

"We have our reasons."

"But, Gerald, I'm not equipped to handle Meg's problem."

Gerald's eyes narrowed. "Don't interfere, John."

John remained quiet for a time. After breakfast they drove east toward the community of Winterboro. Miles down the road, Mulga Cave came in sight. At Winterboro Gerald turned south toward Morrisville six miles away. Before arriving in the community of Paper Town, Gerald swore John to secrecy.

"Megan is pregnant."

John took a deep breath. "Has her gynecologist confirmed it?"

Gerald kept his eyes on the highway. "Yes, the day after the 4th of July. I'm scared for her, John. We've been so careless."

John looked at a distance. A dairy farm came in sight. The large pine trees hid most of the pasture land. "But a pregnancy is not uncommon. You and Megan are ready to be parents." He turned to look at Gerald. "Psychiatric treatments are shorter today than they were twenty years ago. Megan should make the trip to Chicago. I'll go along if you'd like."

Gerald ignored the comment. He pointed toward a trucking company east of highway 21, "We're coming up on Morrisville." The First Baptist Church came in sight. "I was christened there." Passing the turn-in to downtown Morrisville, they continued over Morrisville Mountain. On the east side of the highway the sprawling fifteen hundred acre ranch came in sight. Gerald slowed near the foot of the mountain; turned up a long driveway. John read the sign arched over the drive way; *Nolen's Ranch.*

"Nice area," John commented.

Gerald pointed to a building near the highway. "That's Mother's Clinic."

"So this is Nolen's Ranch?"

"Yes, I doubt we'll find Nolen here. He spends his time in Montgomery working with ABI. Nolen is into law enforcement. The man is in demand."

Gerald stopped in the front yard. Sheila Garcia's Jeep came up the driveway. "Are you ready to sell a few brood cows?" Gerald laughed.

Sheila bounded from the vehicle, her eyes on the visitor. "You must be Mr. Randall," she stated offering her hand.

Taking her hand, his heart pounded. "Yes, Ma'am, I'm John Randall."

Noting his reaction, she moved away. "Where do you want the brood cows delivered?" she asked.

The horrible scars; she looked away.

"I live east of Birmingham. He folded his arms, keeping the scars from her view. Gerald couldn't believe her behavior. He'd witnessed something he preferred to forget. John Randall's appearance upset her.

They walked toward the barn. John's purchase, ten brood cows, stood in a feeder lot. The animals' eyes fell on Sheila approaching. Gerald, eager for his mother to accept John, said. "Mom, are you aware John was a friend of Dad's?"

Sheila gave Gerald a sly look. "Yes, so I've been told." She changed the conversation. The cows would not be delivered until the end of the week.

"Mom, John and my father served together before Dad was killed."

"That happened thirty years ago. I care not to discuss it." She turned to John, "Mr. Randall, if you were my dead husband's friend, why have you waited so long to communicate?"

John, taken aback at her abruptness, told her of the flame thrower. Ashamed of his appearance, he never planned to return to the United States. Gerald, Jr. was trying to help him locate his roots.

Sheila, stared, but said nothing. She turned toward the house, Gerald and John followed. She arrived at her Jeep, crawled in, "Gerald, call me tonight, do you hear?"

She cranked the engine. "Mr. Randall, thank you. Your cattle will be delivered Friday." She turned the Jeep toward the Clinic.

John chuckled. "I don't think your Mom took a liking to me."

Gerald shook his head. "She's a marvelous person. Maybe she and Nolen are having problems."

Chapter 12

September 1983....

For weeks, Gerald endured Megan's unhappiness; nothing seemed to please her. Saturday morning, to get away, he visited John at the farm. They sat on John's back porch, a chill was in the air, they watched the sunrise. John asked about Megan's condition.

"Why would you ask, John? Meg's a bitch at the moment. She can't be happy; no matter what."

"So you're depressed over her condition?"

John hedged, not giving a direct response. "Hell, Megan has to grow up."

"Be patient, Gerald. This is her first child."

"But you'd think she's the only woman to ever get pregnant."

"And you the only man who has this problem," John chuckled. "What about the Chicago trip?"

"Megan says she'll go, if her mother agrees to accompany her for the five weeks of treatment." He gazed into space taking a deep breath, "I want her to go. I need a break."

"You must be tired. How are they traveling?"

"Amanda is flying them." He looked toward the sky, a few clouds appeared near the sun. "You still plan to go?"

John nodded, "Yes, Amanda insists I go for an evaluation."

Thursday morning at 7:15 Amanda's Beechcraft lifted off Sylacauga's runway. She landed in Birmingham, picked up John, her third passenger. The flight to Midway Airport took only a couple of hours. On arrival, Amanda remained at the airport to secure the Beechcraft; John and Dot accompanied Megan to the clinic.

The receptionist looked at Megan as if she had returned home, but stared at John. She eventually asked. "Are you Megan's parents?"

John shook his head, "No, Ms. Sutton is her mother."

The receptionist nodded, "Dr. Gray's expecting you."

John found Megan and Dot a seat. Ted Gray stepped into the room, came to Megan, "So you're back." He nodded, "Where is Amanda?" He eyed John standing near Megan's chair.

"Amanda will be along" Dot stated. "She stayed to secure her aircraft.

Ted turned to the receptionist, "Assign Megan to a room; get Dr. Holder on the telephone."

Gray looked first at Dot, then John, "Are you Megan's parents?"

"No, I'm her mother; John's a friend."

John interrupted, "I'm John Randall."

Ted took John's hand, "Amanda told me you were coming for an evaluation?" He eyed John's face.

John gazed at the ceiling, "Amanda says there are new techniques."

Ted received a phone call; soon returned, looked at John. "Amanda told you correctly. Be here at nine in the morning."

After five weeks of treatment, Megan had made progress. However, Holder could not assure Megan she was well. "Megan, your illness is unpredictable; sometimes incurable. At times the second personality fades into oblivion." Holder wrote on a pad. "You're fine at the moment; you're healthy. You should have no problem with this child."

Ted examined John's scars giving John definite hope. The scars could be hidden by skin grafts; with an estimated recovery of six weeks. John left the clinic thrilled at the news. Ted Gray had to be a medical genius. John didn't immediately schedule the operation; Anoka was ill. He first must return to Japan...

Second week September 1983...

After a short night's sleep, John crawled from bed with much to do before he left for Tokyo. At 9:15 AM he called a cab. The airport was bustling with people, many traveling west to winter Olympics, others going to winter resorts.

He purchased a one-way ticket to Tokyo, not knowing if he would be returning. Anoka's son gave little hope that Anoka would live past the end of the week.

Delta's flight 214 left Birmingham on schedule non-stop to San Diego. John changed planes and hours later walked into the Tokyo terminal; caught a cab to the Tokyo Rose Hotel. After checking in, he took a quick shower and grabbed a bite to eat.

The September evening was chilly with a slight breeze blowing in off the ocean, the cab driver stopped under the hospital's breezeway, John hurried to the information desk. Anoka Faureta was on the fourth floor. Faureta's son, Mitshu, met John at the nurses' station and led him to Anoka's room. Anoka, propped on pillows, looked up when John entered; his eyes were weak.

Moving to his bedside, John reached for Anoka's hand, "Good to see you, my friend."

Anoka's eyes focused on John's face, "Thanks for coming, something I must tell you."

"Not tonight, Anoka, maybe tomorrow."

Anoka shook his head, "No, it must be now."

Anoka asked Mitshu to step outside. With the door closed, he began to talk about their first meeting right here at this hospital. "I worked undercover as a Japanese and American agent. I gathered information during the war." He asked for water, John gave him a sip. "A well known American agent who worked for me was killed in Korea. North Koreans feared the man so we didn't want them to know."

Anoka chose to keep the agent alive in the body of another American soldier; John Randall was the dead agent's name.

John... taken aback. "You gave me Randall's identity?"

"Yes...you are the man."

John focused on Faureta's rugged face. "Then who the hell am I?"

Anoka, tried, but he couldn't recall. "Go to Nikko. Visit the priest at the Shinto Shrine. He once worked for me. He'll give you directions."

John got to his feet, shook his head, "To save the name of a damn dead agent, you made me a sacrificial son of a bitch?"

Anoka's eyes closed, his breathing heavy, "I made a mistake, but didn't expect your mind to ever recover."

John looked toward the ceiling, "So you took it on yourself to become God?" John shook his head; he pounded his temples. "I'll go to Nikko tomorrow." He looked into Anoka's eyes; tears had appeared, "You get some rest."

The train station was crowded. John pushed his way in from one side while Japanese detrained on the opposite side. John moved through the crowd to find a window seat. Checking his watch; it was after 7:00 AM. If Faureta made it through the night, he would be having breakfast. He thought how he should hate the man, but he loved the old bastard.

The trip north to Utsynomia, sixty nine miles away seemed shorter than John remembered. The train stopped a couple of times to allow passengers to board or de-board. It continued on to Sendai, a city much further north. Arriving before nightfall, John chose to spend the night. He would get a night's rest and leave for Nikko next morning.

After John's uneventful night in Sendai, his train left for Nikko arriving in a drizzling rain. John checked in at a hotel, received directions to the Shinto Shrine, ate lunch and flagged a rickshaw. Finding his way to the shrine's front interior, he asked for the head priest. Moments later a short balding man in his forties appeared. He bowed in John's presence. The man had to be Anoka's friend. John explained Anoka had sent him.

"How is Anoka?" he asked, folding his arms to his chest.

"Not well, Sir; he wasn't expected to live through last night."

The priest led John to his office, closed the door, He removed a large book from his library. He invited John to sit while he thumbed through the pages. He found his reference, scribbled a number on paper and returned the book to its shelf. Taking a seat the priest gave John the reference along with instructions to find the military storage section of the shrine's library. Told by the priest to follow strict instructions, John was not to copy a word he read and he had to agree to return to the shrine before leaving Nikko.

The flight of stairs leading to the building's entrance seemed to never end. The building's oriental design, its roof lines were appealing. Inside, a small female sat at a desk. She came to her feet when John entered. She wouldn't dare to look at him directly. John, fluent in the Japanese language began to explain the nature of his visit. Impressed at his knowledge of the language, she led him to a room with a high security safe door. She dialed a combination, allowed him to enter. Following the code he received from the priest, he found a book near a top shelf, opened it to a key page as directed by Anoka. In small print at the bottom of the page, he read about the death of John Randall. Taking a deep breath, his heart racing, a frown appeared on his face. Perspiration began rolling from his forehead.

Words written in Japanese, left John with no doubt, he now knew he was not lying in a cemetery in Morrisville. He now understood the visions, the sandy beach, the North Koreans rushing from a mountain side. He had a wife and a son, God only knew where. Looking back, for months he sensed ties with Morrisville, but never heard of Nolen's Ranch. Closing the book, he placed it back on the shelf and returned to the shrine. The priest invited him in a second time, closed the door and in English stated, "Now you know, Mr. Price. Your service was necessary."

John frowned. "For thirty years, I have lived as another person. How could you?"

"We're sorry, Mr. Price." The priest lowered his head, rose from his seat, "Give my best to Anoka; have a safe trip home."

The two men stared at each other, in a battle of wills; both having silent courage, neither yielding a sign of weakness.

John returned to Tokyo to find that the night before, Anoka died in his sleep. The funeral was short; few people attended. John, already missing his close friend, returned to the Tokyo Rose Hotel. More frustration built inside to know now he did have a family; his true identity was frightening. What would Faureta say? "John, put your mind to work." He decided to remain in the country, bide his time until he could decide what course to follow. He'd spent thirty happy years in Tokyo. Why should he return home? How could he face Gerald? More frustration, how could he face Sheila? He couldn't; he had to think.

For months, he roamed the streets of Tokyo, communicating with old friends he had known for years. A year passed, almost a second. He took a job at the hospital as a therapist. Everyday his heart longed to return, but his intuition kept him as if he were wrapped in a security blanket; Japan was home away from home. Each night he soaked himself in Japanese sake. Before the end of his fourth year, he realized he'd never find happiness until he returned to the United States. A week later, he packed his suitcase, checked out of the hotel; caught a cab to the airport. Delta had his ticket waiting....

Chapter 13

Five years later, August 1988...

Delta flight 114 touched down at Birmingham's airport near midnight. John retrieved his luggage and walked outside the terminal to flag a taxi cab. The late night air had not cooled from the hot August sun, as it swept across John's scarred face. He loved the smell of the states, wondered why the orients were so different. Arriving home, he checked his watch; it was now 1:00 AM. To unwind from his hectic day he went to the kitchen to pour a stiff drink. On the table lay a pile of letters, one in particular, caught his eye; the handwriting was familiar. The return address was Gerald's office. He froze in place for a moment, Megan had disappeared again. But the letter was two years old. John reached for the phone then thought better of it. It was too early in the morning. Gerald would be in bed. The call could wait until morning. He thought of poor Gerald trying to rear a kid without its mother. He'd take Gerald to lunch tomorrow, but for now his tired body pleaded for rest.

Friday morning, after sleeping past eight, John climbed from bed, went to the kitchen, made coffee and prepared toast. After a second cup, he went to the bedroom to place a call.

The phone rang, in Gerald's office. Sarah answered then called, "Mr. Price, on one."

"Thanks, Sarah."

"John Randall, Gerald. I'm back. How are you?"

"What? You're back? You've been gone too long. Hell, we all began to think you had died."

"No, it's a long story. I'll tell you about it later. How are things with you, Gerald?"

"Not good, John, but I'm surviving,"

"Sorry, what's the problem? How's the child?"

"Child? John, do you realize you've been gone five years? We had a second born two years ago. Kids are with their grandmother."

"Dr. Garcia?"

"No, Dot's here."

"Where's Megan?"

"Who in the hell knows?"

"Come on, Gerald, you actually don't know?"

"Hell no, man. She's been gone since Trey turned six months. Not a word. Not a single word."

"Gerald, we need to talk. Can I buy your lunch today?"

John pulled into Britney's. After five years the place was the same; still didn't have adequate parking. His mind drifted to his predicament. Why had he returned? On second thought, Gerald needed him. He'd help find Megan.

They went through the line, took a seat near a front window. Sitting nearby, a strange man stared. John suspected he and his female friend were discussing his scars. The sandals with painted toenails set the man apart.

Gerald under his breath asked, "A homosexual?"

John almost smiled. "I don't know. He's probably a cross dresser."

Gerald nodded. "They're weird. Dot has a niece married to one."

They sat a moment in quietness then John asked. "What about Megan?"

"Not much to say. She didn't leave a note; left the baby in the crib; little Stacey to look after him." He stared at John. "I came home at noon; gone."

"Left her new born?"

"Six weeks old." Gerald nodded. "This pasta and shrimp salad is good, John. How was your trip? Why were you gone so long?"

"Okay, the fact is, stayed longer than I should." He cleared his throat, knowing his comment wasn't fact. "How's your mother?"

Gerald looked up, a waitress refilled his tea glass. "Fine, but why would you ask?"

"Do you object?"

"Should I?"

"What gives, Gerald? I've been gone five years. I merely asked about your mother out of courtesy. You resent my asking?"

"I guess I see the worst in people these days. Sorry, John."

John nodded. "The unknown is tough to take. I'm sure Megan is on your mind." John paused. "Your stepfather back home?"

"Strange you'd ask about Nolen. We buried his father two months ago. You recall meeting, Joe?"

"Don't think I had the privilege."

"Nolen's mother moved in with Mom, but why your sudden interest in my family?"

"Gerald, you're plain edgy."

"You seem different."

John ignored his comment; sipped his tea; looked at the waitress; she brought a refill.

"You think Megan will return?"

Gerald frowned, "Here you go again. How would I know? Not sure I give a damn."

John paused. "Sorry you're in such a foul mood, Gerald."

Gerald paused; gazed outside at the flow of traffic. "I'm not myself." He cringed, shaking his head, "How could she leave the children?"

John felt his pain, "Maybe Melanie left, not Megan."

In the parking lot, Gerald mentioned Columbus. "You still plan to find your family?"

John was in deep thought. "Right now, there's another matter we need to discuss soon."

"Thanks for lunch." Gerald pulled away for downtown Birmingham. The traffic was light for midday. John returned to the farm not certain he'd find a way to untangle his life, not sure he wanted to. Where could Megan be? Gerald's attitude had changed. Melanie had taken control. Meg wouldn't have left her children. Driving up the tree lined driveway toward home a strange vehicle sat in the yard. An enforcement officer waited on the front porch. John parked, made his way toward the stranger. Before John he could speak, the officer stuck out his hand, "John Randall? Nolen Garcia."

John extended a hand, eyeing the visitor.

"Mind if we sit?" Nolen asked. "I'm exhausted."

John led the way to rockers on the back porch, "Could I get you something to drink?"

"No, thanks," Nolen opened a package of cigarettes.

"What brings you to Birmingham, Nolen?"

Nolen laughed, "I'm not here on police business. Gerald tells me you're good at raising beef cattle."

"Yes, but you didn't come to see my herd." John kept his eyes penetrating.

"Did Gerald tell you my father died a couple months back?"

"Yes, sorry to hear it."

"I'm looking for a ranch manager. Think you might be interested?"

John shook his head, "I'm settled in here."

Nolen laughed, "Sheila says you'd be an asset to the ranch. She sometimes is moody; but wise beyond her years."

They walked to John's backyard; to the fountain Megan had engineered. The subject of Megan's disappearance surfaced. John questioned why she left a perfectly good home, a husband and two children.

"It beats me. Sheila wants to bring the kids to the ranch." He paused to light a second cigarette. "Mother is living with us; she'd be the perfect nanny." He smiled. "But Gerald wants them nearby."

"Nolen... thanks for the job offer. I'll discuss it with Gerald tomorrow. Incidentally, where would I live?"

"Do you think we'd expect you to rent?" Nolen laughed. "I spent a fortune renovating a place for my parents."

"What would the job pay?"

"Name your price; we'll negotiate. The ranch consists of fifteen hundred acres. You'll have Bubba Miller, a black man, to assist you."

John thought of haying time, "Extra help during special seasons?"

"Up to you and Sheila; she'll be your supervisor."

Nolen got to his feet. "I have to be in Montgomery by noontime. Shall I tell Sheila you're considering it?"

"I suppose. Gerald will call her tomorrow." John's voice carried over a burst of noise; a jet taking off from Birmingham's airport.

Nolen pulled away; John entered the kitchen; poured a glass of tea. He began to search his soul, more concerned about Megan than a ranch job. His ultimate thought was to locate her; it had to be done. Gerald needed her at home.

Chapter 14

Second week August, 1988...

Friday morning John crawled from bed, made a pot of coffee, dressed for the day. The August sun was already beaming its rays through the kitchen window. His appointment with Gerald was at 9:00 AM.

Arriving at 8:45 AM, Gerald was in the break room. A copy of the Birmingham News lay beside him. "You're early." He looked up, nodding for John to sit. "Can I get you a cup?"

"Thanks. How are the kids?"

"Still asleep when I left."

After coffee, in Gerald's office, Gerald shut the door. "What's on your mind?" Gerald took out a legal pad; called Sarah to hold his calls.

"Nolen came by the farm yesterday."

Gerald grinned, "I'm surprise he'd leave Montgomery. What's his beef?"

"No beef; you'd be surprised what he wanted." John laughed.

"No, to the contrary, I prompted his visit."

"Gerald? You shouldn't have done it."

"But, you'd be an asset to Nolen's Ranch." He dropped his pencil. "And for some reason, Mother feels the same."

John got to his feet, walked to a window, looked down on the busy street below, took a deep breath, "But I don't understand your mother. Remember how she acted last time I was there?"

"I can't say I do. Was I present?"

"Come on, Gerald. Hell, let's not play games. We went there to purchase cattle. She gave me the cold shoulder."

Gerald, with eyes fixed on John, "We all have good and bad days." Gerald called Sarah to bring in more coffee. "Mother, not I, prompted Nolen's visit. John, he could care less about that ranch; the man is obsessed with law enforcement."

"I'm not sure I could please Dr. Garcia." He frowned, "Then too... what am I to do with my place?"

"We'll find a buyer, or you can keep it for weekend visits." Gerald moved around the desk; Sarah brought in coffee. "I'd recommend you take the job and hold on to your Birmingham home. People do have vacation homes, you know. . Your property will increase in value as years go by." He sipped his coffee. "John, Mother needs you and I'd like for you to take the job."

John nodded, in deep thought, "Aren't you being a

bit presumptuous? Why your sudden interest in me going to Morrisville? What am I suppose to do with my therapy practice?"

"It's time you sell that shopping center. If you play your cards right, Mother will pay you well; they've got millions."

John paused, "Millions? They've earned millions running a damn cattle ranch? Come on Gerald."

"No, I'm not kidding. Nolen inherited millions." He cleared his throat, "They'll never spend all their money. Nolen's rich. So, hell man, demand a large salary." He laughed.

"No, I refuse to take advantage of the man." John gave a quizzical look. "Not on your life."

Gerald, with a concerned look, shaking his head in utter disgust. "But you'll be worth it to Mom, John."

Monday morning, third week in August, near 9:00 AM, Dot Sutton opened the front door to retrieve the Birmingham News. She looked up to see a stranger standing at the foot of the steps gazing at her. The man appeared to be of Mexican descent. Dot's heart pounded; a feeling of terror ran through her body. She turned to re-enter when he called to her, "Lady, do you live here?" he asked.

Dot hesitated, "What is it to you?" she asked, a frown sweeping her face. "What are you doing here?"

The man's eyes expressed displeasure, but he kept his composure, "I'm sorry, Ma'am. I'm looking for an attorney who lives in these parts." He turned to leave, "I must have the wrong location."

He moved to his car, Dot called to him, "What's the attorney's name?"

The man shrugged, "Not sure, but he practices criminal law downtown."

Dot frowned, keeping him in focus, "Why are you seeking his residence?"

"It's a private matter, Ma'am. Sorry to have bothered you." He opened the car door, took out a small camera and made a photograph of Gerald's home.

"Wait a minute, Mister." Dot screamed; her frustrated look caught the stranger by surprise. "Who gave you permission to photograph this home? Who are you?"

The stranger shrugged, "I'm in real estate. I mean no harm; we take photos to compare property prices."

Dot glanced toward a sign on his car door. She turned to re-enter. "What's the name of your firm?" He had pulled away.

A week later, John put his therapy practice up for sale. The commercial properties would be handled by a Birmingham rental agency. Sheila agreed to allow him to move his cattle to a north pasture until he could sell them. With an agreed salary John moved into the cozy home beside the road. He would begin his new position immediately. Why he had allowed Gerald to talk him into such a foolish move he wasn't sure.

John spent September with Bubba Miller, baling hay, mending fences, acquainting himself with his new position. They worked each day from morning till night with only a short lunch break. Bubba Miller smiled noting the man Sheila had hired was no stranger to farm work. Sheila kept busy spending her time with animals brought into the vet clinic.

The last week-end of September, Gerald and the children came to Sheila's for a visit. John spent some time with Gerald's kids. He took Stacey to the horse barn to see an aging pony Nolen had given her father when he was a child. Gerald had promised to teach her to ride when she arrived at an appropriate age.

The first week of October, Sheila came by John's house for a quick business visit; several animals had broken through a fence on the backside. She decided they should ride the fences together; clinic business was light on Wednesday mornings. John saddled two horses and helped her mount. John turned to Bubba, "Keep an eye on things." Riding side by side on horse back toward the back pasture, Sheila began to tell John a weird story; an animal once kept the whole community up in arms for five years. John appeared to listen, but his mind wasn't on her conversation.

He interrupted, "Please excuse the interruption, but could we talk about Megan, Ma'am?" John asked.

She cut sharp eyes at his scarred face, apparent anger in her mild voice. "Why would you be interested in my daughter-in-law, Mr. Randall?" Her look alerted John; he'd touched on a conflicting subject.

"Megan is a sick young woman, Dr. Garcia. I doubt she left Birmingham alone." He stopped to straighten a fence post; she waited...

Sheila's temper flared, "But you fail to understand. Gerald gave her the best medical care money could buy." She raised her voice. "He can't live from one day to the next not knowing if she'll return."

"Ma'am, would you mind calling me John?" He mounted his horse.

She said nothing, again headed down the fence row. He followed, keeping an eye out for strays.

Moments later, they arrived near the backside of the pasture. She chose to dismount and walk a spell. Finally, she turned to look at him, "Tell me what you know about the death of Gerald Price."

"Ma'am, do we have to talk about it?" He frowned. "I've spent hours searching my brain about what happened to him."

"I think the truth is... you never served with my husband." She kept her eyes straight ahead.

"Ma'am, I'm sorry I can't be more explicit, but yes, I did serve with someone I think was he."

Suddenly, she changed the subject, "Would you be receptive to working at the clinic sometimes, if I needed you?"

John almost grinned, looking in her direction. "Ma'am, if that's your wish, but I'm not trained in your field." He nodded. "With Dr. London there, why would you need a ranch manager to assist?"

She stopped near a stream running through the pasture, "Let's let them drink." She removed the wide brim hat, shook her hair loose; looked at him. "Often I need help when I treat large animals, John. Is that difficult to understand?"

"Hold it, Dr. Garcia. I didn't intend to be rude; certainly not questioning your authority." He frowned, looking straight ahead. "If we're going to work together, at least we can show mutual respect." He looked toward the distant mountains. "However, I refuse to be a target of your unhappiness, Ma'am."

She watched her horse drink, didn't look up. "You're quick to pass judgment, Mr. Randall." She turned, a half smirk, half smile appeared on her face. "I didn't mean to offend, Sir, but my happiness or unhappiness is none of your business."

"I'll keep that in mind. Ma'am, I'm here at your

request. Gerald thought I was needed, but if you'd like, I'll return to Birmingham."

She looked at him a long moment, he was serious about leaving; she needed him here. "I think we understand each other, Mr. Randall. Is there anything else we should air before we continue?"

"One thing, Ma'am, I would like for you to understand that Gerald is like a son. I've learned to respect him and his family. I would like your indulgence in finding Megan. I promise my efforts will not take me away too long."

He helped her mount. They rode south toward Mahee Creek. She didn't give him the courtesy of an answer. A flock of Canadian geese took flight from the lower pasture. "Those things are going to create a problem," she stated.

"Ma'am, they'll move on in a day or so." He looked up, "Mind if I ask a personal question?"

She hesitated, "If it's not too personal."

"Have you visited Gerald's grave site lately? I'd much like to see it sometimes."

Sheila pulled her horse to a halt, dismounted, walked to the fence separating the ranch from the main highway. She looked at him, "There's something about you that puzzles me, John." She pushed hair from her eyes. "I can't put my finger on it."

He nodded a slight smile appeared on his scarred

face, "You're curious about my coming to work here? Is that such a mystery?"

"No, first you ask time off to find my daughter-in-law, which is ludicrous. Then you want to visit Gerald's gravesite. I have a problem with that. You claim not to remember him. Why would you care to visit the place where his body lies?" She kept her eyes fixed on his.

"Forget I mentioned it." His apparent irritation showed.

She came closer, "You commented earlier, it's essential we show each other respect. Why are you so irritated?"

"Have I been disrespectful?" he asked.

"No, you haven't, but for no apparent reason, we have difficulty understanding each other." She looked at her watch. "It's time we return. I have to be at Barnes' Dairy after lunch."

John rubbed the horses down before releasing them into the pasture. He returned home for lunch before he and Bubba Miller went back to baling hay. When 6:00 PM came, they returned to the barn; a tall man, in his early forties, was waiting.

The man dunked a cigarette, "Are you John Randall?" he asked.

John nodded, "I am."

"Sir, Gerald sent me to find you. He wants you to come to his office right away."

"Is Gerald in trouble?"

"Sir, I'm not privileged to the state the nature of his business, but its urgent."

John turned to Bubba. "If I'm not back by daylight, you feed. Will you look after things?"

Bubba nodded. "I'll tell Miss Sheila where you've gone."

"Thanks, Bubba." John looked at the stranger. "Tell Gerald I'll be along in an hour."

John rushed home, took a bath, changed clothes, and headed for Birmingham. Over Morrisville Mountain he headed north, passed Paper Town, he turned left at Winterboro. An hour later he pulled into the parking lot at Gerald's office. The night watchman allowed him to enter. He took the elevator to the third floor. Gerald was sitting behind his desk, his eyes red; he'd been crying.

"What's happened, Gerald?"

"It's the children...my children have been taken."

"What? When did this happen?"

"Dot fed them supper, dressed them for bed. A Mexican man and woman appeared, locked Dot in a bed room and grabbed the kids."

"Have you reported it to the authorities? Gerald, kidnapping is serious business."

"John, hell I'm an attorney. I know what I'm up

against." He frowned pulling a handkerchief from his pocket. "But why would someone take my kids?"

"Money my friend, I'd venture they want money."

Gerald walked to the window, looked down on the busy street below, night had fallen on the city. "I'm not a rich man. Money isn't their motive."

John listened, taking a deep breath, "Maybe it's Nolen's money."

Chapter 15

Second week September 1988....

At 8:30 PM Gerald called Birmingham's detectives to report the kidnapping. An immediate bulletin went out to enforcement agencies. By 9:00 PM, Sheila arrived at Gerald's office. She began to blame Gerald for his slow action in reporting it to authorities. John resented her reprimand. "Just a minute, Sheila, this is no time to place blame. He's in pain." John's eyes glittered.

The nerve of this hired hand; he'd never called her Sheila before. He wasn't acting like an employee; a ranch manager. He was assuming the role of Gerald's father. For a moment, his quick response took her aback. She said no more, but a thought entered her mind. Could she permit this kind of conduct? She needed him at the ranch.

Nolen Garcia sat behind his borrowed desk in the ABI office working to find yet another clue into the five year old murder of a female whose body was found in the Alabama River. The telephone rang in the front office, the secretary called to Nolen, "For you, Mr. Garcia."

Sheila rushed to tell him about his grandchildren. He abruptly stopped her, "Sheila, I know. We received the bulletin. We're on it already."

She said nothing for a long moment. He waited, "Sheila, you there?"

"Yes, I'm here, Nolen." Her voice carrying a cold tone he felt in his soul. "Why haven't you called?" she asked.

He paused, collecting his thoughts, "I called...have you talked to Mother since you left the ranch?"

"No, I expected you to contact me here; Gerald's office."

"You're over reacting, Sheila. I had nothing to report."

"It's time that you put an end to your ego trip, Nolen. You'd best make your way back to the ranch. I'm tired of carrying the workload of the clinic and the ranch."

"I can't leave for a couple of months, Sheila. I'm close to solving a hideous crime. Shoemake would hemorrhage if I dropped it now."

"Okay, you have till Christmas; five years away is long enough, Nolen."

Nolen paused, "Don't threaten me, Sheila. You've never hurt for a thing since I accepted this project. I don't take a liking to being told what to do."

The phone went dead, "Sheila?"

Four days after the children were abducted, Gerald's phone rang. Gerald reluctantly picked up the receiver. John Shoemake from ABI was calling to say a state trooper near Dallas, Texas stopped a Mexican for a tail light violation. He noted two Caucasians, a boy and a girl were sleeping in the car's back seat. A Mexican female sat holding a small boy in her arms.

Gerald got to his feet, "Did he arrest them? Where are the kids?"

Shoemake interrupted, "No, he had no reason. The children are still in their custody."

"Surely he got a tag number. Was it a Texas tag?" John paused.

"No, Arizona, the vehicle was registered to a Stanley Wilson. Sorry I can't provide more, Gerald. We'll be in contact."

Gerald turned, shaking his head, "Two children fitting the description of Stacey and Trey were found in the back seat of a Mexican's car near Dallas, Texas." Gerald moved to the water fountain, drew a cup, "A Mexican man and woman; God only knows where they're headed."

"I'm surprised the trooper let them go."

Gerald called to ask Nolen to keep him informed on any further developments. Nolen stated an alert had already gone out to all western states describing the couple.

John Randall crawled from bed at 4:00 AM; ate a light breakfast then headed to the big house. He rang the doorbell and Sheila answered dressed in her robe. "Isn't it a bit early for you to visit?" she asked.

"Sorry to disturb you this early, Ma'am. Would you consider allowing me to be away for a week?" He hurried to assure her Bubba could handle the ranch until he returned.

"You've only been here a few months and already you need time off?" She frowned. "I'm disappointed you even ask, Mr. Randall."

John nodded. "But, it's for your family I'm making this request, Doctor." He looked up at the sky, rubbing the back of his neck, controlling his emotions. "I'm going to find your grandchildren and bring them home."

"But that's a police matter, Mr. Randall. Let them handle it, for God's sake." She brushed her hair from her eyes, evident frustration penetrating her being.

John kept her in focus for a long moment, nodded, "Sorry I bothered you, Sheila. Obviously, you don't give a damn what happens to those kids." He turned toward the steps; she called to him.

"Wait...how long will you be gone?"

"Not more than a week; maybe ten days at the most." He kept his eyes fixed on hers. "I'll get back soon as I find them."

She stepped outside to the porch noticing the morning sun already casting a bit of light on Morrisville Mountain. "Do you need money?" she asked folding her arms to the morning chill.

"I can manage, thank you. Do I have your permission to go?"

She paused looking directly into his eyes, "If I say no, would it make a difference?"

He smiled, "Thank you, Ma'am." He nodded. "I'll be back...you'll see."

When he got to his car, she called, "John, be careful. I need you here."

Bubba drove him to Atlanta. John approached the desk at Delta Airlines. The drive to Atlanta seemed to take forever. He purchased a ticket for Salt Lake City, picked up an Atlanta Constitution and waited for board call.

Service personnel mingled throughout Atlanta's airport. John thought of his old friend Faureta, the one person who had made his life in Japan worth living. He wondered what advice Faureta would give him. Suddenly, a voice on intercom called his flight. With his carry on baggage, he waited his turn for clearance to enter the aircraft.

Gerald Price, Jr. contacted Sheila by phone at 7:30 AM to tell her about a call he had received from John. He couldn't believe the man would go on a wild chase trying to find the children. "He's chasing the wind, Mom. Did he say where he was going?"

"No, and I didn't ask, Son." She paused awaiting his reaction; none came. "He was adamant about finding my grandchildren and shamed me into agreeing."

"But, Mother, you should have stopped his insanity!" Gerald paused. "The man has no idea what he's doing!"

She nodded smiling to herself. She thought of John Randall. There was a twinkle in his eye, a resonance in his voice, a determined look; he'd succeed, if it were possible. "Gerald, the man's will to find my grandchildren dominated my decision, so let him try." Her voice quivered.

Gerald hung up convinced John either had information as to where the children had gone or surmised a plan to find them. With no better plan of his own, Gerald decided it best to bide his time; John Randall was trustworthy.

The September skies over Salt Lake City were set in a sea of blue, not a cloud in sight. The pilot announced they would be on the ground in 10 minutes; stewardesses moved down the isles checking seatbelts. Within minutes, the runway seemed to bounce into plain view; the pilots glided toward the eastern end. Moments later, John felt the touchdown bounce then came the whirl of the reversed engines to cut the aircraft speed. When the aircraft came to a halt; the pilot maneuvered to an unloading position.

John retrieved his baggage, not having the slightest idea where he would be going. He caught a cab to the Temple of the Latter Day Saints. He walked up the steps, entered and there before him the Mormon Choir was preparing to do a television program. Nearby he spotted a small office and decided to enter. A young attractive female sat behind a desk. John's approach caught her attention. She looked up. "May I help you, Sir?"

John cleared his throat, "Could you direct me to your library?"

She studied John's face, the scars distracting. "There's a directory near the door, Sir, but you'll find the library in that building across the street."

John searched the files for a Stanley Wilson. Wilson had been excommunicated from the church after being arrested in July 1983. The Governor Howard Pyle had ordered an investigation of a community known as Short Creek. Wilson was guilty of being married to a fourteen year old child along with five other wives. The man served time and was released from prison. The file said nothing about his present whereabouts.

John learned that LDS members who continued polygamy after the Mormon Church disavowed the practice were permanently excommunicated.

John asked the clerk on duty in the library if they had a record of where excommunicated members lived.

"Are you seeking to find Mr. Wilson?" she asked. She suggested he search through old newspapers at the Salt Lake Tribune. "Sir, Wilson's name comes to mind, but I can't recall the incident." She frowned. "I believe he got in trouble with the law back years ago."

John found his way to the paper where he gained permission to study old 1980 news releases. He searched headline after headline until he found an incident in September 1981. Stanley Wilson kidnapped a fourteen year old girl from her home in Salt Lake City. She remained missing for two years. At the time, Wilson was a married man with several wives who lived in Arizona. John made notes, but also had a photo-static copy made of the article. Leaving the newspaper office, he checked in at a downtown motel where he placed a call.

"I'm in Salt Lake City at the moment."

Gerald gave a sigh of disgust, "What do you think you're doing?" John tried to speak, "No, you listen, John, you're poking your nose into police business and you could get your ass killed. Give up this wild pursuit and get back here; Mom needs you at the ranch."

John, persistent not giving in, began to give reasons why he was in Salt Lake City. "I'm no crackpot nor am I chasing the wind. I'm on the track of the son of a bitch who has your children; don't ask me for the impossible."

Gerald took a deep breath, "You're onto something? What's this all about?"

John paused, took the pad from his briefcase, turned to where he had scribbled "Wilson."

Gerald again attempted to get his way. "John, I appreciate your efforts, but come on home."

"Sorry, I made Sheila a promise I'd find her grandchildren." He cleared his throat, "Remember Mexicans had the kids and were driving a car with an Arizona tag? The owner's name was Wilson."

"Leave it to the FBI. They're looking into it."

John changed the subject, "Call Doctor Garcia; tell her this could take a few more than 10 days. I'll talk to you later."

"John?" The phone went dead.

Silent Courage

Chapter 16

Three days after arriving in Salt Lake City....

After breakfast in the motel dining room, John read an article in the Salt Lake Tribune that caught his attention; it told of a religious sect in Colorado City. But the place was located in Arizona. The writer told how Colorado City was once known as Short Creek; renamed a few years back. Wilson came to John's mind. Wilson could be living in Colorado City; Megan might be there under the spell of a polygamist bastard. The article spoke of how Fundamentalists practiced polygamy, had large families, many living on welfare. The city was located on the Arizona Strip, a particle of land northwest of the Grand Canyon, a corner of Arizona ostracized from the rest of the world, separated not only by the Canyon, but also by a hundred miles of dusty desert. The article stated the place was controlled by the head of the Fundamentalist Latter Day Saints Church.

John returned to the library. He had to learn more about the Fundamentalist. Was Stanley Wilson associated with the sect? With no doubt a large family, maybe several wives, why would this man want to kidnap two children in Birmingham, Alabama? John's mind raced; there had to be a reason. He sat at a table in the library and concocted several theories. Only one made sense; Megan was under the mental domination of a Mormon polygamist; she wanted her children brought to her. No law enforcement reasoning would ever make such an assumption.

After a night's rest, John went to a local automobile dealership and purchased a used 1976 Volkswagen. He had the vehicle serviced, equipped with new tires, bought an atlas and checked out of his motel. Leaving Salt Lake City, he headed northwest.

Near mid-night he stopped at Candy's, in Colorado City. He purchased a snack and asked directions to a motel. The waitress, eyeing the stranger, directed him to speak with the manager. She quickly informed him that, in Colorado City, only certain people were allowed to speak with strangers. John nodded, "Thanks for the tip."

With his suitcase that contained a change of underwear and a clean shirt, John checked in at the Comfort Inn near the Municipal Airport. Tired from his day's travel, he decided to retire for some rest.

Hildale, Utah and Colorado City, Arizona are like twins. The two towns melt together with only a street separating them. John learned that Hildale, known for its polygamist population, fits the same mold as

Colorado City. He ate breakfast in the motel's dining room and read the daily news. In a second, John learned the Fundamentalist Latter Day Saints Church controlled every facet of the community. The women who waited tables wore long sleeves with no make-up. The slight blond hardly more than sixteen came to his table.

"Coffee and toast, please," John paused, looking at the menu. "Do you happen to know a man named Stanley Wilson?"

She wrote his order on her pad, nodding, "Yes, I know him, but I'm not allowed to talk with strangers, Sir." She smiled.

John watched as she moved quickly to serve customers. In his mind, he saw Megan in the throes of the FLDS, captured like a spider in a web. After five years she would be brainwashed, not willing to leave; not sure of her own identity. He must find out the facts, gather information from this clannish society, but how could he find the key to open a door slammed shut by a man claiming to get divine guidance personally from God. The whole town seemed to be mesmerized under his umbrella of fear; citizens followed him without question; afraid he'd cast a spell of damnation on them sending their souls straight to hell. John picked up a copy of a skimpy newspaper in the motel lobby. Reading only the headlines he realized this media was designed to plant Fundamental Mormonism into the minds of the community. No doubt left to uncover, the head of the church ran this community. Stanley Wilson, the man who owned the automobile driven by a Mexican; the culprit who probably had Megan in his custody; the perpetrator who stole Gerald's children must be a member of this church. With his heart churning full force, his determination matched with an unending will, John knew he had to find a way to penetrate the shield thrown up by the President of the FLDS. He smiled to himself. There was a simple solution; find a disgruntled excommunicated member who had an ax to grind. That particular person would be among either the lost boys who were excommunicated years back or a female who wanted freedom. The FDLS President worked to keep the polygamist society in balance. The Salt Lake Tribune article mentioned a place which many boys had taken refuge. The majority were teenagers plucked from the church flock like weeding a field or shaking shaft from gathered grain. The church's leadership used flimsy excuses for their act. These men were either, not following the President's rules, or they were dating a female without proper consent. John suddenly realized how he had to shift his strategy. He'd focus his attention on Hurricane, Utah. Megan and the children could be there. He had to locate a cooperative excommunicated church member.

Checking out of his motel, he stopped at a service station, filled up, purchased a local road map and turned northwest on state highway 59. He'd check in at the

Comfort Inn in Hurricane before scouting the place. The desk clerk may be of help.

The date on a newspaper showed he'd been gone from the ranch for four days; time was of the essence; he'd call Sheila tonight. He ate a light lunch and drove to a local bar. In the mid-afternoon, the bar looked much like a bar in Birmingham except locals were wearing cowboy attire. John ordered a drink. Looking into the mirror over the bar, John saw a middle aged female standing near his back staring at him. He turned; she nodded then disappeared into the crowd. An hour later, the female appeared a second time; said nothing, but stared. He watched her disappear through a side door; he decided to follow. Opening the door, he came into a restroom lobby, two restrooms, male and female. The female waited to enter. In a quiet voice she murmured, "Come to my house tonight by nine. I live at 217 West Street. Park away and walk in. I'll be waiting."

John nodded, entered the men's room, jotted down the address, flushed the commode, re-entered the bar. Was he approached by a prostitute or could she be the answer to finding Megan and the children? She singled him out for a reason; he must follow her instructions. He kept in mind Gerald's caution that he could be killed.

Chapter 17

Near 3:00 PM, John left the Comfort Inn motel, drove north, making his way to a nicely kept residential area. The houses were built on well defined acre size lots. Scouting the area, he noted an important factor, no street lights. He decided his best bet would be to walk in under cover of darkness. After he scouted the neighborhood he returned to the motel to plan his strategy. Checking a map, he found the city had been well laid out in streets both north and south. A railroad ran parallel to the back of the home where the woman lived. He'd walk down the railroad and enter through the back door.

John spent the remaining daylight hours reading about how Hurricane came into existence. The town's history was fascinating. He learned that people who came to Hurricane thought they could grow cotton. He was amused at the thought of a certain area in Utah being called Dixie. The homesteaders were successful at growing cotton, but their efforts failed because of the erratic flow of the Virgin River. Their cotton was swept away. John thought of home, wondered how the ranch was doing, He thought of his farm near Birmingham and its red soil. He learned that when the cotton venture failed, it prompted the 1893 digging of the Hurricane Canal; a project involving a cooperative effort by citizens of Hurricane. He was amazed at how each member of the co-op received deeds to 20 acres of land outside Hurricane and one an a fourth acres in the city; a lot for building a home. He nodded his head; now he understood better the city's layout; thoroughly planned before building had begun.

Before 7:30 PM, John placed a call to Gerald in Birmingham. Gerald's line was busy; he waited then placed it again.

"I'm in Hurricane, Utah. What's going on?"

"Where's Hurricane; I'm not familiar with the name." Gerald chuckled. "What on earth are you doing in that place, John?"

John didn't mention his newly made friend Ruby, "I'm of sound mind, my friend. I'll be back to you in a couple of days." He paused. "Have you heard from Sheila?"

Gerald fought his first inclination; John and Sheila were adults; and why shouldn't John call her by her first name? "She's fine. Nolen is either obsessed with his own importance or he's found another woman. He should get his butt home."

John paused, "Nolen's a busy man. Leave him be, Gerald. The man is doing the best he can." John changed the subject. "Have you heard from Megan?"

"No, why would you ask?"

John kept his composure; fought the urged to give him a tongue lashing. "Sorry I asked." He took a deep breath, "You could be more civil. I'm on your side, Gerald."

"Then get your ass home, John. You're flirting with your own death."

Gerald waited. The phone clicked. "John?" No answer.

October 10...

Near 8:45 PM John left the motel, parked in a shopping center parking lot, ducked into darkness and headed northwest on the railroad tracks. In darkness he hurried along finding his way till he arrived at the brick house on the corner lot. A light was burning in the bedroom; a dim light in the kitchen. Easing his way forward down through a mass of heavy grass he crossed an empty ditch to arrive at a wire fence. Suddenly a flash of light sprayed the area; he froze ducking into the tall grass; breathing heavily; the light vanished. Moments later he arrived at the back door, gave a light knock, she appeared, he ducked inside. She cut the kitchen light, led him to the bedroom; closed the door.

"She held his hands; they were shaking, "It's all right; you're safe here. I'm Ruby. I want to help."

John breathed a sigh of relief, "Do you know why I'm here?" he asked.

She nodded, moving to the window to scan the outside. "Yes, we have kept an eye on you since the day you arrived. We assume you're here because of Megan's kids."

John shivered with excitement. "Megan is here? You know where the children are?"

She frowned, keeping her eyes focused. "We know she's nearby all right, but I'm not sure she's ready to leave."

John thought long and hard. Megan was here; the children were with her; that was most important. The rest was secondary; he'd find a way to communicate the importance of her leaving; Gerald needed her at home.

Ruby sat on the side of the bed with her hands folded in her lap, "I'm risking my life, but women must escape this mad man's prison." Tears welled in her eyes. She told him of her own plight as a 14 year old, forced to marry her own kin whom she despised. She escaped her cousin's household, spent time in the desert country with members of the Paiute tribe. After ten years the Paiute's helped her return to Hurricane under an assumed name. A year later, she assembled an organization known as the Underground Railroad for the purpose of helping young girls escape to freedom. Her source of assistance came from young men who had been excommunicated from the church in Colorado City.

John listened, eventually interrupting, "Do you know Stanley Wilson?"

"Yes, he is the prophet in the church; a powerful man who claims he communicates directly with God." She offered John something to drink; he declined. "He owns a large peach farm in Washington County; has a home in Colorado City; married to four or five women." She shook her head, "Why would you ask about Wilson?"

John selected his words, still reluctant to trust Ruby. "His car was used to transport Megan's children from Alabama to Raton Pass." He hesitated. "State Troopers found the car abandoned. Evidently, the Mexican couple who stole the children had an accomplice to pick them up by aircraft."

Ruby brought in a bottle of wine, popped the cork and poured two glasses, "It's him all right. He owns a couple of helicopters and a light fixed wing plane. He has his own runway near the peach farm. I'm told he travels extensively in pursuit of business prospects." She downed a gulp of the wine, "But how could he have induced your Megan to come here?"

John paused, remembering how Megan was sick, a dual personality who, at times did not know what she was doing. "It's a long story, Miss?"

She smiled, nodding, downing the remainder of her glass, "My friends call me Ruby; that's it; I'm just plain Ruby."

"Ruby it is, Ma'am." John frowned looking at the floor; his mind fixed on getting Megan and the kids out of Washington County. "Can your railroad help me to get Megan and the children to Salt Lake City?" His eyes showed deep pain. "Would I be safe to pick them up there and drive across country?"

She came to his side, sat down near him, placed her hand on his, "I know the pain you feel; how eager you are to take them home, but Mr. Randall..."

John kept his eyes fixed on her. She shook her head, "Chances are, Megan will never leave Wilson alive." She paused; poured a second glass, "You see, he sends his women to a brainwashing clinic north of here. It's a way of punishing them for wanting to leave. Your chances of her going home are slim; I hate to say."

John's eyes pierced hers; a look of fear appeared on her face. "I'm going to take Megan and her children home, Ruby; with her permission or without it. Will you try to talk her into coming to Salt Lake; maybe for some event; make up a reason Megan will buy."

She leaned forward, touching his hand, "Can you give me a day or so to try?"

Near 10:30 PM, John slipped through the back door, worked his way to the railroad; walked back to his car. He and Ruby agreed to meet a second time; same place in two days. She agreed to communicate with Megan, but not to inform her about John's presence in Utah.

He returned to the Comfort Inn, picked up a sandwich and entered his room. Tired from a busy day, he flicked on the news; took a quick shower. Tomorrow he'd call Amanda Sims....

The calendar on the kitchen wall reminded Sheila that John had already been gone ten days. It was now the middle of September. Why was she so eager for him to return? A thought crossed her mind. Nolen would be coming home to stay by Christmas. She glanced through the window. Why was she worried? Bubba Miller was doing well at finishing up haying season. The ranch was doing well. But Bubba missed John. Each day he would ask when Mr. John would be back.

Gerald came for the week-end; his heart heavy, he longed for his children. But in reality, he missed Megan as well. Saturday morning Sheila prepared Gerald's favorite breakfast of egg benedict, bacon and toast. The phone on the kitchen wall rang. Gerald picked up the receiver.

"Amanda Sims, Gerald. We must talk." She paused. "Could we meet some place for coffee?"

Gerald, taken aback, with no reason to think responded. "Yes, what about little Sam's at nine?"

"Fine, come alone if you don't mind." She cleared her throat. "See you at Sam's."

Hanging up, Gerald poured a second cup of coffee; looked at Sheila, "I have to go into town for a while; should back before noon."

Sheila's keen mind took control. "This quick trip... does it concern the children?"

He frowned taking his time, sharing her concern. "I'm not sure, Mom, but we'll talk when I return."

Gerald drove to the back parking lot at Sam's to find Amanda sitting in her car waiting. He quickly held the car door for Amanda, she dismounted. They turned toward the entrance. Gerald asked, eagerly, but with cautiousness," Is this about Meg?"

They took a corner table, "Yes, Gerald, it's also about John. I received a telephone call from him and I think he's onto something. We couldn't discuss it over the phone."

Gerald felt his pulse beat faster, his eyes narrowed; he took a deep breath. "Has John found my children?"

Amanda, not sure, refrained from generating hope. "I can't answer that; he didn't actually say." She frowned, looking into Gerald eyes. "He placed a heavy request on me, Gerald. I felt you should know." She told him of their conversation; how John had gone to Hurricane, Utah, made contact with someone who wanted to help. "Gerald, he thinks Megan is living on a ranch with a family of Fundamentalist."

"What about the children?"

"He says the children were brought to Utah at Megan's insistence. What her relationship is, with the polygamist community, I wouldn't venture a guess." Amanda called the waitress; ordered a sweet roll. "I think John Randall is flirting with danger. I've heard that the law in the area works for the church's President; he controls everything, even who the young people can date."

"Why did he call you, Amanda?"

"He wants me to fly Megan and children out, if the Underground can arrange it."

Gerald's mind was now filled with every conceivable thought. "Underground? I don't understand."

"Not sure if I can explain it, but John says it's an organization operated by people who are unhappy with the Fundamentalist Mormons; men and women who are victims of abuse."

Gerald nodded, beginning to see the concept. "What's your thinking, Amanda? How many can you fly in the Beechcraft?"

She could handle John, Megan, and the two children without difficulty. One additional passenger would not overload the aircraft.

"But, Amanda? This would place stress on you."

She frowned, nodding. "Yes, it's an imposition, but what are friends for?" She paused. "Gerald, we'll talk about the cost after we've flown the mission."

"But think of the hours you'll lose!"

"No...you think of getting your children back." Her voice was clear, her mind made up. "We have to try."

The telephone rang twice before John reached for the receiver. Amanda had called to say she must have specific instructions to file a flight plan. "John, this is touchy so don't let poor planning screw it up."

John assured her he would search for pitfalls before he allowed her to fly to Utah. His main concern at the moment was timing. A mix-up could be fatal to the mission. She agreed.

John got out of bed at 6:30 AM to find an envelope on the floor at the door. He picked it up noting no address. He opened it to find inside a short note from Ruby directing him to her home by 9:00 PM. She gave no clue; no information; only the short message.

Leaving the motel near 7:45 PM, he walked along the railroad tracks, keeping a low profile; he'd arrived near 8:45 PM. The high grass near a peach orchard made an ideal cover until it was time to enter. At 9:00 PM sharp he stepped to Ruby's back door; knocked. Moments later, the latch clicked; she motioned him to enter.

"I've located Megan and her children," she announced. "They were not where I expected." She paused, drinking from a wine glass.

John, excited kept his emotions hidden. "But you have found them?" He asked.

"Yes, Megan's been living for almost five years among the Paiutes on a reservation near the Virgin River."

Ruby told how Stanley Wilson had found Melanie, whom he had once met in New Orleans, in a Birmingham tavern and talked her into coming west with him. He brought Melanie to Colorado City to live with his family on his peach farm for a month. Then Melanie began to act strange, calling herself Megan. "This Megan wasn't the same sweet little thing Wilson found in Birmingham. She fought back." Ruby laughed. "Yes, Sir, she was high spirited. She gave Wilson so much hell he thought he had brought home Satan."

The Paiutes took Megan in after Wilson threw Melanie out into the cold. John learned the Paiutes found Megan roaming the streets of Hurricane sick with pneumonia. Weeks later, Stanley Wilson decided God had sent her to him for a reason. She must become his sixth wife. Wilson's informers found she was living among the Paiutes. Wilson sent for her, but the Indians suddenly couldn't speak English.

John listened, still not convinced Ruby could be trusted, "But the children...who stole the children?"

Ruby walked to the window, pulled the drapes tight. "A Paiute couple decided to make Megan happy. So, they stole a car from Wilson."

"But we thought they were Mexicans."

"They could pass for Mexicans." She frowned. "What's your interest in finding the children, John?"

John sensed she doubted his motives. "I'm a friend of their grandmother and their father as well."

She looked deep into his eyes, "How can I be sure? You might be a member of the Fundamentalists with your own ulterior desires." Her eyes were a cold steel gray.

"Ruby, you can talk to their grandmother, if you'd like." John's eyes met hers; he attempted to cover the scars.

Ruby wrote Sheila's telephone number, "Will she accept my call?"

John nodded, "I'd suggest you allow me to introduce you to Dr. Garcia."

Ruby dialed, the phone rang twice, Lori, Nolen's mother answered. Sheila was at the clinic; she gave her the number. Ruby called the clinic, Jack London answered. "It's for you, Sheila."

Ruby handed the receiver to John, "Sheila, I'm in Hurricane, Utah."

She interrupted. "Your time out there is up, John Randall."

Her cold words rang in his ears, "Okay, I understand; explain later." He paused, "Sheila, talk with Ruby; she's trying to help. Will you tell her why I'm here?"

Ruby took the phone, "I'm just Ruby. Is this man for real?"

Ruby smiled, "Thank you, Doctor." John took the receiver, "Yes, Doctor?"

"There's nothing happening here that can't wait a few more days." She paused. "Bring them home, John."

Ruby looked into the mirror pushing her hair away from her eyes. "I've received information that's not good. Wilson's people are searching for the girl." She flipped a lighter to her cigarette. "At the moment the children are safe." She looked directly at John, "We've got work to do."

Chapter 18

Third week September 1988...

John left for the motel with Ruby's plan ingrained in his mind. It was simple enough if she could get the Paiutes and the Jackson brothers to cooperate. Ruby had known her Indian friends for years; the Jackson brothers, former members of the FLDS, she had to trust. One plus in their favor, they held a grudge against Wilson. The Jackson brothers had been excommunicated from Wilson's church. Ruby was well aware that her Paiute friends didn't care for the Mormons. The Paiutes, like their fathers before them worshipped the wolf or followed the teachings of a prophet who called himself Wovoka. The man took on the name Jack Wilson.

"I suppose he's Stanley's relatives?" John asked.

Ruby laughed, "No way, John. Stanley isn't Indian."

The next day passed with no contact from Ruby. She took her time to communicate with both the Paiutes and the Jackson brothers. From past experience she knew Wilson would avoid trouble with the Paiutes. Her Indian friend Gray Wolf and his wife lived outside Richfield near Hurricane. Gray had managed to obtain a HUD house built years before.

Amanda's bedside telephone rang. She flipped on the lamp, looked at her watch. It was near mid-night. She recognized John's voice.

"Sorry to call so late, Amanda, but I need your help." He sounded desperate. "In a day or so, could you fly us out of here?"

Amanda now wide awake, "Have you found them?"

"I haven't seen them, but they're here." He cleared his throat. "I want you to fly them home." Amanda chuckled, "John Randall, you're an idiot, you know that? But I love you for what you are doing."

John kept the receiver to his ear; returned her chuckle.

"What's your target date?"

"Then you'll consider it?" John asked.

"Do I have a choice?"

John thanked her; he'd call again in a couple of days. He asked that she treat their conversation private. Fundamentalists in Colorado City could change his plans. Again he apologized for calling at such a late hour. The phone went dead. Amanda used the bathroom, got a drink of water, checked her watch again. Ted Gray would die if he knew what she was planning to do.

John read in the Utah Tribunal that during Jimmy Carter's reign as President, he signed legislation restoring Federal recognition to the Paiute tribes. The Paiutes tribe was granted more than four thousand acres of land scattered throughout southwestern Utah. The government also provided a grant of 2.5 million to help the Paiute's deplorable economic conditions. Before the grant, many Paiute women took jobs doing house work, heavy motel room cleaning and serving as maids in more affluent households. Paiute men took factory jobs. Wovoka's ghost dance continued to claim the minds of many, especially among the elderly. Ruby assured John her Paiute friends could be trusted.

It was now September 24th. Sheila checked the calendar. John definitely was over due, but he was dependable. He promised to return with the children. How could she doubt him?

The telephone rang in John's motel room. "John, Ruby, it's time to move."

John's heart beat increased, "Should we meet some place?"

"I think not. No need taking chances." Ruby paused. "Your pilot must land at Cedar City Regional tomorrow night by 11:00 PM. Have her fly in from Salt Lake City. Hurricane is closer, but no lighted field. We must load the cargo quickly. The controller on duty will be a Paiute. He'll cooperate."

John hung up and called Amanda. It was time to bring Gerald's family home. Megan's leaving Utah had not been discussed, but the assumption was she'd gladly return home.

Amanda got up early, ate cereal, slipped into a flight suite, checked the time. At 7:00 AM she filed a flight plan. The light travel bag fit snugly behind the rear seat. The flight would be long, but John was expecting her. Bunk Nabors had the Beechcraft ready for takeoff when she arrived. The first leg would take her to Memphis. Anniston Flight Service predicted the weather to be nice except bumpy round Salt Lake City. In Memphis she topped the tanks off a second time, called for a second check of the weather round Salt Lake City. She decided to wait until she arrived at the Salt Lake City airport to communicate with John.

Chapter 19

September 25th...

The cool September day had a slight breeze blowing in from the Northeast. Ruby crawled into the passenger seat of John's 1976 Volkswagen near 7:30 PM. Traffic in Hurricane had begun to slow, street lights were already on. With John at the wheel they headed northwest to Kanosh's Indian reservation. In route Ruby gave John information about the Indians he would meet. The Paiute tribe first occupied the reservation in 1929 after the Federal Government gave them the land. Since that time, Paiute families had survived in small mud huts with few modern conveniences. The community followed their leader, a thirty three year old strong willed Paiute who lived by the rules of the big brother, "The Wolf," a leader who kept his sights on modern technology. Ruby talked of her many friends in Richfield.

Near 9:30 PM John and Ruby arrived at the reservation. Ruby gave John instructions directing the way to Gray Wolf's home located out from Richfield near the Virgin

River. It was late, but Gray's wife, a plump small woman, who did Gray's bidding, had dinner waiting.

After dinner Ruby began their meeting. "Gray, the rescue party must be on time." She paused. "Can I count on it?"

Gray nodded, looking first at John then at Ruby. "Ruby..." he pondered. "Does Wilson know? Will we have to murder the son of a bitch?"

"I pray not." She frowned, "It's a possibility, but Gray, why would you ask?"

Gray Wolf mulled her comment. "I have no reason, just a thought. Count on it. I'll have your passengers in the shadows." He eyed her, she smiled.

John wasn't sure what Gray meant. He had to trust Ruby's judgment. He wondered if Gray would bring both Megan and the children, but dared not to ask. Ruby knew Gray Wolf; they were partners in the Underground Railroad. Their attention to details told John this wasn't a virgin voyage.

Before leaving for the Cedar City Airport, John and Ruby stopped at a local service station for gasoline. At a second pump nearby Ruby recognized a big burly man; a Wilson family member. John paid for the gasoline and immediately they returned to the highway.

"John, the man at the gas pump is Wilson's oldest son." She paused. "There were two others in the car. This could be trouble, but I'm sure the Jackson brothers have them under surveillance."

John kept his eyes on the road, occasionally scanning the rear view mirror, "They're coming our way." He checked the mirror again; Ruby turned to look out the back window.

"Turn right at the next road up here."

"But I thought we were going to Cedar City."

"We are, but let's see if they follow."

John turned right on county road 24; moments later, the sedan followed. Ruby suggested they continue to the next small town. They crossed a railroad leading into a community. A train's lights flashed on the crossing, the engineer activated the whistle; the sedan was forced to halt. John, already across pulled to a stop in the rear of a large store building....

Amanda waited for a phone call at the Salt Lake City Airport. She grabbed a quick bite to eat, used the rest room and returned to wait outside the phone booth. It was now 9:45 PM. She again checked flying time to Cedar City; the field would be lighted; the Paiute said he would recognize Al XYN Code 4. A phone rang in the telephone booth. Amanda jumped up to answer. The voice, mellow, quite appealing said, "Amanda, I'm Gray Wolf's brother and I'm on duty until mid-night." He paused. "You must be prepared to leave on a moments notice."

Amanda took a deep breath, "I'm waiting for instructions." She managed, frustrated at the long wait. "When shall I leave?" She asked, "This is Code 4."

Without hesitation, the voice said. "Soon, standby, you'll be notified."

Gray Wolf under cover of darkness, left home in a small Honda heading northwest paralleling the Virgin River until he came to crossroads. He stopped, cut his headlights, blinked them twice and waited. Out of a large gorge on the right side of the dirt road silhouettes of three bodies appeared in the moonlight. Not a sound was made, the small child began to whimper; the mother covered his mouth with her hand. Gray quickly opened the door; Megan and the children got in. Megan took the back seat with Trey; Stacey sat in front. Gray cranked the engine and slowly moved through the intersection to find a place to turn around. Moments later he was on the main highway to Cedar City. Megan finally asked, "Where are you taking us?"

Gray Wolf in broken English explained that they were to be picked up at Cedar City Airport by a plane from Alabama.

She choked back tears. "Who are you, Sir?" She asked.

Gray told her of his association with a lady named Ruby who developed an organization known as the Underground Railroad. "We work to save young women caught up in the practices of the Fundamentalist Church."

Gray kept his eyes straight ahead. "They may try to stop us at the airport. You and the kids must remain with me until your plane is on the ground."

"But why are you doing this?" Megan asked. "Stanley Wilson is a Godly man. He wouldn't hurt a soul." Her voice quivered.

Taken aback at her comment, Gray kept his emotions under control. "Ma'am, are you sure you want to return home?" His voice conveyed his true thoughts. "We're interested in helping women who want to leave. Are you convinced you want to go home?"

"Yes, Mr. Wolf, but will God punish me for leaving? I'm confused by all I've been told."

Gray Wolf frowned hearing her remarks. Ruby once told him of a place north of Hurricane, a stronghold of Fundamentalists who punished members when they failed to do Stanley Wilson's bidding. "Have you visited the camp north of Hurricane, Ma'am?"

Megan's temper flared. "I haven't been brain washed, Mr. Wolf. I'm of sound mind and I believe God punishes people who failed to do Stanley's bidding."

Gray Wolf scanned the highway ahead, dimmed his lights, quickly cut into a short road behind a grove of fruit trees. He stopped, cut the engine, "Look, Ma'am, we're not risking our lives for some bitch who wants to live with a man who has a bunch of women under his control." He cut his eyes in her direction, the children said nothing. She looked in his direction then out the window, tears welling in her eyes.

"We thought you were being held hostage by Wilson; that's why my brother and his wife stole you away." He frowned, keeping his eyes fixed on hers. "What gives with you, Ma'am?" he asked.

Megan wiped tears away, took a deep breath. "I'm not well, Sir." She ducked her head wiping her nose with a handkerchief.

"All right, I'll help you get away from here, but don't hand me that crap about Wilson being a saint; he's a no good son of a bitch, Ma'am." He nodded. "He's raped more young Indian girls than anyone in this territory; I've thought about killing him."

"I'm ready to go home, but I'm not sure I'll stay." She dropped her head then looked up. "It's best I go home for the sake of the children."

Gray Wolf nodded, "And it's best for you too, Ma'am." He cranked the engine, "You'll feel better once you're back in Alabama; I'm sure of it."

Arriving in Cedar City, Gray Wolf turned onto the two lane highway leading south adjacent to the airport. Two miles later, he found his familiar parking place near the end of the runway. He and Ruby referred to the place as the shadows. The area, a peach orchid with trees still covered with leaves. He pulled the vehicle between two trees so close the doors could hardly be opened. He, Megan and the children waited. He swore them to silence. The only sound they could hear were frogs croaking in a small pond near the end of the runway. An airline aircraft's engines roared lifting the passenger plane off the runway. Gray Wolf got out of the car and made his way to a position near where the Beechcraft would land. Suddenly he detected an unusual silence in the area. Thus far, there was no apparent sign of Wilson's party. Then it happened, car lights flashed from the west. The car was on the opposite side of the runway. Like semi fore from two ships a second car flashed its lights from the north sending a return signal. Gray's mind raced. He had seen these signals before. He thought of every conceivable scenario. Wilson had his henchmen waiting to grab Megan and the children. He couldn't allow them to be exposed. The idiots were capable of trying to disable the aircraft or capture the pilot. His mind filled with various possibilities. Surely the Jackson brothers would be arriving soon. They could act as a decoy, lead Wilson's men on a wild goose chase; take them away from the airport.

From a distance, Gray heard a car engine coming, but there were no lights. The car moved slowly in darkness. Only Ruby and the Jackson brothers knew about the shadows. John's Volks Wagon turned off the main road and headed in Gray's direction. John pulled the car under the cover of two large peach trees before he cut the engine. Not a sound except for frogs croaking in a distant pond. John and Ruby dismounted and slowly made their way into the peach orchard. Against the skyline they spotted the silhouette of a vehicle. Ruby whispered, "It's Gray."

"The kids are awfully quiet," John stated.

"They're probably asleep." She touched his arm, "Wait here," she whispered. "Gray and I have a call sign." Ruby moved ahead a few steps and made the sound of an owl. She did it a second time; an owl sound returned. Gray Wolf was there all right. John and Ruby moved into Gray's location. John, for the first time in five years found himself in the presence of Megan Price. He couldn't see her face, but recognized her voice, "John, why did you come?" she asked.

"For heaven sakes, Megan, you're going home." He cleared his throat, "You okay?"

"Why do you ask?"

Megan was different, a stranger, not the person he knew five years ago. "What's your problem, Megan?" He asked. "You're different."

"Different?" She smirked. "I'm different thanks to Stanley Wilson. He's a man of God."

John struggled to control himself. "Stanley Wilson?"

"He brought Melanie and me here from Birmingham." She said in a soft voice. "Well, it was Melanie's idea."

"But you've been living among the Paiutes." John frowned. "Why?"

"Years ago Melanie made Stanley angry." Her voice quivered.

"I found myself all alone. I was taken in by this Paiute family. Melanie, the mean bitch left me. I haven't seen her in four years."

"That's good news, Megan. Maybe she's gone forever."

Silent Courage

Chapter 20

John left the party in the shadows to find a telephone. He had to call Amanda in Salt Lake City. He drove to the south end of the runway and made his way to the main highway. Moments later he darted into a parking space at the airport, quickly entered, found a phone booth. He instructed Amanda to keep the aircraft's engines running. They would cross the airfield in Gray's sedan, load Megan and children and she could be on her way.

"You're not coming, John?" she asked.

"I'll be along later. Tell Sheila I'm driving through."

John made his way to the east end of the parking area. Three of Wilson's Fundamentalists were waiting. He drove by their vehicle capturing their attention then sped away south at a high speed toward Hurricane. He watched in the rear view mirror. As he expected, they followed. Their pursuit of John would take them away from the airport. Amanda arrived at Cedar City on schedule, touched down; taxied to the far end of the field, turned to taxi back to the terminal. Suddenly, she pulled the aircraft to a halt and opened the door. Gray Wolf sped from the orchard to the runway with Megan and the children. They dismounted the vehicle and Amanda lifted the children on board, Megan crawled into the co-pilot's seat. Amanda slammed the door. She cautioned Megan and the children to buckle up. She taxied to the end of the runway. Gray Wolf's brother recognized her call sign and directed her to take off when ready. Moments later, Amanda lifted off, veered southeast toward Memphis. She climbed to 25,000 feet, leveled off and cut back on the engines. She turned to Megan and invited her to put on the headsets. The children in the back seat were already asleep.

John sped along highway 59 southeast toward Hurricane, but suddenly the Volkswagen engine began to labor; the high altitude had taken its toll; the men in pursuit came closer. John could no longer move away. At the next service station he left the main highway. The station wagon with three husky members of Wilson's Fundamentalist family moved in to block him from entering the station. They approached the Volkswagen, the taller man, known to the others as Josh, reached for the door on the driver's side. John tried desperately to start the engine to no avail. Suddenly, the three moved away from John's car and waited...

Ruby and Gray Wolf came to the airport, but John wasn't there. Gray Wolf searched the parking lot for the Volkswagen, circling the terminal several times, "He's a man of courage," Gray suggested. "Wilson's men may kill him."

Ruby suggested John had performed the Jackson brothers' job. He led Wilson's men away from the airport. "That's why we had no trouble." Ruby shook her head. "Gray, we must find him."

Amanda landed first in Oklahoma City for fuel and proceeded to Memphis in the wee hours of morning for a second re-fueling. Topping off her tanks, she called the tower for take off instructions and continued her flight plan to Birmingham. Once in the air she turned on the radio; Megan and the children were asleep.

A news bulletin flashed, bad weather was moving into Alabama. She immediately called the National Weather Service for additional information. Stacey waked up wanting to use the restroom; Amanda convinced her to hold it; she'd land in Huntsville in fifteen minutes. She called Anniston to report her short stop in Huntsville.

Gray Wolf and Ruby headed south on highway 59 searching for a trace of John. Which direction he had taken was only a guess. One thing was certain... he was being followed by Wilson's gang. Eventually they reached a 24 hour service station with bright lights glowing and John's 1976 Volkswagen sat at a pump. "Thank God, he's here." Ruby offered, directing Gray to pull in beside the Volkswagen. Ruby bounded from Gray's sedan and made her way inside. An elderly woman operated the place.

She sat dozing in a rocker, an Indian blanket to keep her warm. When Ruby entered, a bell attached to the door jingled. The attendant looked up to see Ruby, but said nothing, waited for Ruby to speak. Ruby asked about the man who owned the Volkswagen at the pump outside. "He left with three men; didn't pay for his gas." She got to her feet. "I expect him back for his vehicle."

Ruby's mind raced. An image of what had happened to John, caused chills to her body. "Did you know the men who took him?" she asked.

The woman walked behind the counter, shaking her head, "Did they take him? Lady, I don't know everyone who buys gas." She yawned, "And, Ma'am, it's 2:00 o'clock in the morning. Did you get some gas?" She asked, not caring to continue the conversation.

Ruby, irritated at her manners, took a deep breath to control her temper, "No. I did not."

The woman scratched her head, turned with a crude look. "Let yourself out."

John waked in the back seat of a Ford sedan strapped like a prisoner between two overweight men. It was early morning. The sun had begun to rise. At a distance, he saw what appeared to be, an American flag flying above a large building. It seemed to take forever, but as they came closer, he realized he was heading for a building that sat inside a chain linked fence. John worked to gain his composure; to grasp knowledge of where they were taking him. His sense of direction told him they were in a desert. As they approached the building, his judgment told him they were taking him into confinement; a prison; a holding area. Stanley Wilson was going to place him in prison without a trial. Wilson had to be a madman, his power generated in the name of God.

The sedan pulled up to the gate, a lone guard in khaki uniform wearing a jungle hat, approached.

The driver pulled a card from his pocket, "We have an intruder who needs a place to stay."

The guard laughed, motioning the vehicle forward. The driver continued to the front of the building. The grounds were kept to perfection. At a distance men and women as well, were bursting what appeared to be rocks. The driver ordered him out of the vehicle; the men in the rear seat push him along toward the entrance. Inside the place looked much like a civil court room. No one spoke until Wilson's three henchman approached. Behind the counter a large female stared at John. "Why is he here, Josh?" She asked the taller man to John's left.

"He's being charged with assisting a member escape." The second man interrupted, "Wilson wants him punished."

The female nodded, wrote on a pad, "What's his name?"

Neither knew so Josh punched John, "Tell her you're name, man."

An hour later, John found himself in a courtyard with two other men. They approached him appearing friendly, "You must be Mr. Randall," the taller man said.

The second interrupted, "Randall, you haven't met us, but we know you. We're the Jackson brothers; he's Milt and I'm Rick."

"You guys know Ruby?" John asked. "What are you doing here?"

Milt looked at Rick then at John, "Long story, certainly not to our liking." Milt took a look toward the guard shack, "We've been on Wilson's "Wanted" list for months, a bit of car trouble did us in. Big Josh found us on the side of the road; that's it."

John moved to the back fence, looked out across the desert land, not a living thing in sight. "How long will they hold us?" John asked.

"Hell, who knows?" Rick kicked up a clod of dirt. "Big Josh says we're headed for the mines."

Chapter 21

Amanda radioed Anniston Flight Service to inform them she would be landing in Huntsville for thirty minutes. In moments, Huntsville Airport's landing field came in sight. She touched down and taxied to an unloading point, waked Megan and the children. They made their way to the terminal, used the restroom and returned for a bite of food in the restaurant. Reloading her passengers, Amanda called the tower and moments later the controller gave her permission to take off; once in the air she notified Anniston she was in the air again on her way to Birmingham. She asked for an update on the weather; receiving a favorable report for the Birmingham area.

John lay on the canvas bunk in the open barracks with only a GI blanket to cover his body. With windows standing open, the gentle night breeze blew in warm air that became colder as mid-night approached. He awaked at 3:00 AM with a thought in mind. He had to get back to the ranch; Sheila was depending on him. He had to find a way out of Arizona. His only hope was Ruby and the Underground Railroad; they must be aware of this hideous hell hole in the desert. He got out of bed, eased quietly into the restroom, took a badly needed leak and started to return; no lights were on. Suddenly, he spotted the profile of someone heading in his direction; he moved to the side and waited...

A voice sounded carrying throughout the building, then came a whisper, "Randall, I'm Molly, a friend of Ruby's, a part of the Railroad. I work here; underground. You do as you're told until I can contact Ruby."

John felt his heart quiver, he could hardly believe the large lady whom he had seen the day before was a part of Ruby's underground, "Ma'am, I understand. What about the Jackson brothers?"

The gruff female voice, a bit irritated, whispered, "Worry bout you own ass, man. We'll get them out in time."

"Thanks, Molly. Good advice."

Molly indicated that the next contact she made would be the night before he would be joining Ruby and Gray. She cautioned John not to reveal her position or to discuss the Railroad with inmates. Wilson had informants planted among the workers.

At 06:00 AM big Josh came through the barracks shaking bunks screaming to the top of his voice, "Be in ranks outside in 10 minutes."

John rolled from the lower bunk, scampered to get

his pants on, put on his shoes and headed for the door buttoning and tucking his shirt. It was evident that Josh once had served in the army. Josh marched the group to a small building near the rear. They were served red beans and cornbread; no coffee, only a tin cup of water. Josh rushed them to finish.

After breakfast, the work crew of eighteen men mounted the back of a flatbed truck. The driver headed southeast further into the desert. They traveled at high speed along a road of packed sand. Josh would not allow the prisoners to talk. He required them to sit at attention; look straight ahead.

An hour later, an open pit mine came in sight. No one aboard the vehicle dared to ask questions or look in the mine's direction. The driver stopped, Josh commanded they dismount, fall in a line. He led them to the mine and divided them into teams of three. John was held responsible for keeping his two team mates busy. In a moment, they determined they were here to mine uranium. Each man received either a pick or shovel. By nine, the sun was sending its rays directly into the pit. With no wind stirring, before noon, the temperature mounted to more than a hundred degrees. The prisoners received a cup of water each hour. By noon John and his team, the two Jackson brothers' bodies were pleading for shade; the only shade near was a canvas tent mounted near the mine. The tent served as a kitchen. Here, they received their lunch consisting of a bologna sandwich, made by placing the bologna between two slices of white bread; water was provided in a ten cup. The afternoon was no different from the morning; the sun still showed no mercy on the workers and Josh kept his whip drawn to keep the work force in line.

Arriving back at the prison near dark, the prisoners were led to an area near the rear of the building where makeshift showers had been arranged using large oak barrels with a trigger mechanism to release the water. Each man was allowed two minutes to cool and clean his body with his clothes on. Milt Jackson received three lashes from Josh for removing his shoes. John and Rick would comfort him once lights were out.

Chapter 22

Three nights later, John made his trip to the prison latrine at the same hour, 2:00 AM. On his return trip he spotted the silhouette standing in view. It was close to the hour of his departure; she had assured him he'd be leaving, he never doubted the power of the Underground Railroad. Ruby was the brains behind the train and John respected her judgment. He moved light footed to a corner in darkness, the silhouette seemed to follow. He stopped in place and waited...

Molly came closer, touched his hand, "John, Ruby said to tell you to have a heat stroke in the mess tent tomorrow." She whispered, "Make them remove you to Hurricane's hospital."

"What if they refuse?" John asked.

"Damn it, John, you should know we have no guarantees."

John told her to tell Ruby he would do as she asked, he'd make it a grand performance.

Morning seem to rush in. Immediately after roll call, Josh forced the prisoners to take a short run to the mess facilities. Breakfast of baked beans and corn bread was served with water. Rushing through the meal, the prisoners were allowed ten minutes to brush their teeth, use the bathroom and be standing in formation to move out for the mine. Rick was the last out of the barracks and received the crack of Josh's whip to his back. Milt's temper flared, but John kept him in tow.

At the mine, each three man team took its place receiving their pick and shovel. Each team began its morning toil with a short break at ten. Josh allowed an extra cup of water, an unusual feat John realized he had not done before.

Lunch time came and he marched them to the tent where the cook served each prisoner a bologna sandwich and a cup of warm water. Suddenly, for no reason John Randall created a commotion. He fell to the ground shaking as if he were having a seizure, his eyes rolled back in his head, he groaned. Josh became excited, called for the flatbed truck and ordered John taken to a hospital in Hurricane, "And Charlie," he ordered. "You stay with the son of a bitch until he can return."

Twenty miles into the trip, the driver and guard came upon a helpless female stranded in a black sedan. She had the hood raised on the vehicle. In her hand she held a white handkerchief, waving to the approaching vehicle.

"What have we here?" the guard asked.

"Some damn female must be traveling alone in this

god forsaken place." The driver shook his head. "Females, God, females!"

The driver pulled along side her sedan, she frowned. "I think the engine ran hot. Can you help?" she asked, wrinkling her brow.

In a flash, two Paiute Indians raised up from the sedan's back seat, armed with rifles. They pulled the driver and guard from their vehicle, removed their shoes and forced them to start walking back toward the prison. The Paiutes pulled the sparkplug wires from the truck and left the area with John Randall in the back seat of their sedan. They drove for hours without a word. John didn't say a word, familiar with Gray Wolf's tactics. This had to be the work of Gray Wolf and Ruby and their underground friends. Five miles into their trip, the driver pulled to the side of the highway; the female got out; in Paiut language they said their goodbyes. They drove away leaving the female to take a bus home.

Finally, the man sitting next to the driver, in broken English said, "We're taking you to Salt Lake City then you will be on your own."

John couldn't question the efficiency of Ruby's organization. He decided before arriving in Salt Lake City that he would drive his Volkswagen back to Alabama. John reluctantly asked the Paiutes if Ruby would be in Salt Lake City.

Neither of the Indians knew of a woman by that name.

At 6:45 AM the sun came over the horizon in the east, the Paiutes continued downtown to a room at a Comfort Inn. Without explanation, they led John to a special room. Ruby was there to welcome him. She frowned, "You've been playing with fire, my friend. You could have been killed."

John nodded, swallowing deeply, "Thanks, Ruby, I can't believe the efficiency of your underground."

Ruby smiled, rolling her eyes, but keeping John in focus. "Thanks, but let me say, we don't operate from a position of weakness." They went to the dining room for breakfast.

Ruby turned, peering at others in the room. "Amanda landed in Birmingham yesterday." She nodded, keeping her dark eyes fixed on his. "Oh yes, your boss said for you to get yourself back to the ranch."

"Ruby, I left my car at a service station on the road to Hurricane. I plan to drive it home. Think I might get it back?"

Ruby sipped coffee, looked across the room at the waitress, motioned for a refill, mulled the question, "No, we can't risk it." She wiped her mouth, "Wilson has your car at his peach farm." She lowered her voice, "He expects you to come for it."

John frowned, gave her a familiar grin. "He'll get his wishes. I'm not leaving Utah without it."

Ruby began to shake her head, looking up at the ceiling, "John Randall? You would risk your life for a Volkswagen? You are one stubborn son of a bitch." She shook her head, "I won't take any more chances to save your butt, my friend." She pushed away from the table. "The underground wasn't formed to help stupid men do super stupid things." She moved to the cashier's counter. John took the tab from her hand, "It's mine." After paying the bill the two walked to the lobby. "Wait, Ruby, I appreciate all you've done, but I'm not leaving without my vehicle."

"I know, John, I know." She reached for his hand, "Good luck. If Wilson catches you fooling around his farm, you'll be buried in his cemetery." Ruby walked out the front door, the two Indian drivers waited...

After checking in at the Comfort Inn, John placed a call to Nolen's Ranch. Jack London answered. John asked if Sheila was in. Sheila, visibly upset at John took the receiver. "Okay, how much longer?"

Her coldness he recognized from their youth. "I left my vehicle near Hurricane. I should leave in a couple of days."

Her demeanor changed, something in her voice was different, she was crying. "Thanks, John. You hurry home."

He paused, hardly knowing how to respond, cleared his throat. "See you soon." The phone went dead.

John sat for a moment, thinking of the Underground. Ruby put her faith in two reliable groups, men excommunicated from the Fundamentalist church and the Paiutes. The most reliable Paiute he could think of was Gray Wolf, but would Gray risk his life to help him recover his vehicle? He dismissed the idea; Gray Wolf was too busy with the Underground. But Ruby held the Paiutes in high esteem; she trusted their judgment, admired their courage.

Next morning, John went to breakfast in the dining room and picked up the morning paper. It was now the 28th of October. He had been gone more than ten days. He'd promised Sheila he would return right away. Time was becoming a factor. After breakfast, he checked out of the motel, walked to the local bus station and caught a Grey Hound to Hurricane. He must find a person in Hurricane who could help him recover his Volkswagen.

The weather was chilly outside Hurricane's bus station. John retrieved his luggage and flagged a taxi. Moments later, he checked in at the Travel Lodge, found a telephone directory and called Gray Wolf. Gray Wolf's wife answered.

John recognized the Indian's crisp voice, "This is Gray."

John quick not to irritate, ask if he knew of a dependable Paiute who owned an automobile, looking for work.

Gray Wolf grinned. "You've returned for the vehicle?"

"Yes, it belongs to me and I plan to drive it home."

Gray took a deep breath, "You're a stubborn man, John Randall. You could be killed. Give it to the son of a bitch."

John mulled the thought. "No....Wilson's no God, Gray. That vehicle is my property and I'm taking it home."

Gray agreed to pick him up in the motel lobby in forty minutes. Gray's wife would prepare dinner and they would talk about it. The phone went dead. John took a quick shower, changed into his last clean shirt, turned on the evening news and waited. Thirty five minutes later, he and Gray Wolf were on their way to Richfield.

Gray Wolf insisted John spend the night, had his wife to prepare John's bed in a back bedroom. The only room in the house heated was the front bedroom. The Indian woman piled quilts on John's bed.

Next morning after breakfast, Gray Wolf led John to the bank of the Virgin River. They walked south along the bank and Gray told John the story of how his tribe contributed to the construction of a canal that brought irrigation water to lands near Hurricane. From Gray's comments, John learned that the Paiute tribe had struggled for survival through the years; the US Government eventually recognized their dire need and allotted them a parcel of land. Gray's story was interesting, but John had one thing on his mind, regaining his vehicle and heading home. Sheila needed him.

Gray came to a large rock the size of a small house overlooking the dingy waters below, "Let's sit for a spell." He took a seat on the rock, motioned to John. "If we are to risk our necks for that vehicle, John, we'll need help."

"We can't do it alone?" John asked.

Gray Wolf tossed a rock into the waters, not looking in John's direction. "No, I think not. We must row away from the rocks."

John mulled Gray's strange comment. The man was brilliant; it had to have a meaning. John nodded, "We stay clear of undue trouble?"

Gray looked into John's eyes, "Stay clear of Wilson's men." He stood, wiping his forehead with a handkerchief. "We'll go to the mine tomorrow."

John was taken aback by Gray's comment. "....to that damn prison?" He began to shake his head. "Isn't that rowing into the rocks, Gray?"

"Yes, but we can't go to Wilson's ranch alone." Gray's dark eyes buried themselves into John's scarred face.

They started the walk back to Gray's home, the morning sun beaming its rays over the land, the red soil reminding John he needed to be at Nolen's Ranch. The day went fast at Gray Wolf's home. Gray Wolf showed John his plan for removing John's vehicle from Wilson's ranch. It wouldn't be easy, but the plan should work. They went to bed early with plans to rise early and leave Richfield before dawn.

Gray Wolf's wife cooked them breakfast, packed Gray Wolf and John a lunch. Traffic on highway 59 west was sporadic. They left well before the sun came up over the eastern hills. An hour later, the service station where John left his Volkswagen came in sight. Except for the bright lights surrounding the pumps, the place looked abandon. Gray pulled up to a pump for fuel, John entered the station to pay. Seated in a rocker, the attendant looked at John, got to her feet, moved behind the counter. She checked her register, "You owe ten for the gas you purchased last time you were here."

John frowned; the woman remembered him, why? He paid for the gasoline and turned to leave, "Ma'am, do you know who took my vehicle away?"

She stared at him shaking her head, "No." She put the money in her cash register. "I mind my own business, Mister."

John returned to Gray Wolf's sedan. A few miles west they took a sand filled road to the prison camp. Soon as they left the service station the attendant picked up the telephone receiver. Josh had to know the man with the scarred face was headed in his direction.

Gerald Price, Jr. celebrated the return of Megan and the children, taking them to dinner and a movie. Stacey loved the animated character created by Walt Disney. "Bambi" had just arrived at the Ritz the week before. Trey and Megan as well slept through the movie, Stacey cried when Bambi's mother was killed. Gerald held her close assuring her it was only a story. Returning home when the movie was over, he tucked the children in bed and for once he felt his life was back together again. Going into the living room he found Megan crying. His heart felt for her, but he had difficulty understanding her grief. "What's wrong, Meg.?" He knelt by her chair, "You're not happy to be home?"

"I'm not at home, Gerald Price! This is not my home; it's yours." She burst into tears. "I found happiness in Arizona and you have snatched it away. I hate you, Gerald. I honest to God hate you."

He tried to comfort her, explaining she had gone through a traumatic experience, brain washed by Wilson's church. She shook her head, tears flowing, assuring him she wasn't brain washed, but found a life with a Prophet of God. If Melanie had not appeared, she would still be with Stanley. She and the children must return to Wilson's ranch.

Gerald got to his feet, walked to the kitchen, called his mother. Something was not right, Megan was different. She wasn't the same person he had known five years ago.

"She actually wants to return to Arizona? Has she lost her mind?"

"I can't say, something isn't right. "

Sheila took a deep breath, "You call her mother. Maybe Dot will come to Birmingham for a few days. Son, it's not wise to leave her alone with the children. In her mental state, she might leave again."

Gerald poured a glass of milk and returned to the den, Megan still in tears. She looked at him; he offered to get her something to eat; she refused. He decided to reason with her, try to determine her inner feelings, but he wasn't trained in that field. How he wished John was here...

October 31, 1988....

Gray Wolf pulled to a halt five miles from the prison camp. He carefully drove over sandy soil to a position hiding the sedan behind a large sand dune. He and John dismounted and moved to an observation position near the top of the dune. Gray pointed toward a truck approaching two miles away. "It's Josh and the prisoner going to the uranium mine." He looked a John. "We will shoot out a tire, take the Jackson brothers, and leave the bastards stranded."

John marveled at the Indian's keen sense of fighting. Gray knew Wilson didn't care to make enemies of the Paiutes.

The truck approached laboring to pull the sand dune hill slowing to a crawl the wheels spinning on the soft

sand. Gray took an accurate aim at a front tire; then a rear
one; both bullets slammed into the tires deflating them,
causing the vehicle to halt. Gray moved to a position near
the truck and ordered the driver and Josh to dismount. He
directed the Jackson brothers to take Josh and two other
guards' weapons. The brothers acted quickly and came
to Gray Wolf's position. Gray ordered the prisoners to
dismount and run down the road toward the prison. Josh
started to object only to find a Molotov cocktail flying into
the truck's cab. Josh and the driver cleared themselves
from the burning vehicle and joined the prisoners. John
took it all in from his position behind the sand dune.
Gray Wolf had done it. He'd actually rescued the Jackson
bothers and routed Josh and the other prisoners, driving
them hundreds of feet from the vehicle. Josh called to
Gray, "We'll kill you for this you Indian son of a bitch."
Gray said nothing, but directed the brothers to get into
the sedan's back seat. The four men sped toward Hildale,
Utah. Gray and the brothers had experience beyond
John's wildest dreams. The three seemed to take joy in
harassing Wilson's Fundamentalists.

Chapter 23

Arriving near the edge of Wilson's ranch, Gray pulled into Wilson's peach orchard, his vehicle not visible in the trees. He cut the engine and waited, keeping his ears open to a sign of someone approaching. They would wait here until mid-night when everyone on the ranch would be sleeping. Gray spread the party out having them to establish observation positions. If Josh and his men arrived, they would quietly move out in the opposite directions from which they approached. If Josh didn't show up by midnight, Gray and the two brothers would go on a night reconnaissance, find the Volks. Gray cautioned that if Josh was expecting visitors he would more than likely have a couple of his men sleeping near the vehicle. Gray would be the leader of the patrol.

Gray checked his watch, it was near twelve midnight, Josh and his men had not found them. He eased in darkness to each of the Jackson brothers' position motioning for them to follow; John acted as a rear guard, keeping his eyes trained on the rear of the four man column. They hiked across a grain field, crossed over a wire fence, and moved to a well defined hedge row behind a large barn. Gray motioned the party to halt. He called them together and whispered, "Stay here till I return." No further instructions were needed. John and the brothers didn't question the Indian's plan.

Gray, taking his time, sure footed, making no sound, found his way to the corner of the barn. Neither end of the barn's open area was gated; animals lay on straw near the center. Gray's eyes found a way of piercing the darkness; there near the far end sat John's Volkswagen. Suddenly he heard a noise; someone lay sleeping in the hayloft above. Evidently, Josh was expecting them; he counted on John coming for the vehicle. Gray returned to the fence line...

Dot Sutton arrived in Birmingham before mid-night to find Gerald and Megan sitting in the den talking. She greeted them, made her way to her room, unpacked her suitcase, put on her night gown and returned, "Gerald, would you please bring me a glass of wine? She plopped down on the couch, not yet addressing Megan. She got to her feet and turned off the television, looked a Megan, "We're going to have a talk that's way overdue, Honey."

Gerald returned with her wine, offered Megan a glass, she refused. He came to his chair. Dot would be asking Megan questions.

Dot began to talk about Megan as a child, how she had gone the limit to give her a good education, was proud of her until she finished college. "Since the day you graduated from Birmingham Southern, you have been nothing but trouble to Gerald and to me." Her temper flared, Gerald asked that she lower her voice, the children were asleep.

Megan listened, tears welling in her eyes, looking directly at her mother. She had nothing to say; she listened.

"You are the luckiest female in Birmingham, Megan, married to a wonderful father of your children, have a beautiful home, even a maid to do your house work, a nanny to keep your children, yet you are an ungrateful bitch and I'm ashamed to call you my daughter."

Gerald cautioned, "Dot, don't be too rough on her. She's been ill."

"I'm sick of her illness, Gerald. She has to stand on her own two feet and take responsibility for rearing her two children; no more of this feeling sorry for herself, getting your sympathy, she damn sure is not going to get mine."

Dot finished the glass of wine and ordered another; Gerald obliged. Megan continued to sniffle like a punished child. She waited until her mother had finished her lecture then she began to tell her how happy she had been living with the Fundamentalists in Arizona. Dot immediately countered, "You admit going into a polygamist relationship with some idiot who calls himself a prophet of God, knowing he is married to no telling how many women?" She turned to Gerald, "I think it's time for us to see about having her committed to an asylum."

Gerald looked at Dot, nodding his head, "Could be that she needs time in a mental hospital."

Megan quickly counteracted, "No, I'm not insane. My mind is healthier right now than at anytime since I was born. I know I might sound insane to you, but I'm at peace with myself."

Dot walked to the fireplace, turned to look Megan in the face. She wheeled to face Gerald, shaking her head. "Let her go, Gerald, let the bitch return to her crazy life among those people, but I'll see her dead before she takes the children out there."

Gerald, nodded, his eyes expressed his feelings, he suggested they sleep on it. He had a heavy day tomorrow. He chose to take a separate bedroom. Megan went to her room and closed the door...

Gray eased round the hedge row where the other three members of his party were waiting. Lying flat on the ground with their heads together he told them what he had observed then he presented his plan.

"We will put John inside the Volkswagen and push it from the barn without a sound. If we awake the men in the loft, we'll have to either kill them or they will kill us."

Milt suggested his brother take the steering wheel since he was much smaller than John. They all agreed. Moments later, the party followed Gray across the field to the back side of the barn. Hearing only the snore of men sleeping in the loft, he motioned them forward. One at a time they made their way to the vehicle. Rick Jackson took forever to open the door on the driver's side. He eased inside, closing the door, but not completely. The other three began to push, the Volks move slowly but quietly, from its position away from the barn, down a dirt road leading past the ranch house. Hundreds of yards from the main ranch home, a single lane dirt road used only by work hands, led to the main highway. Rick Jackson took the road, got out of the vehicle and helped push while he guided the vehicle along. Soon they arrived at the main road.

John hurried to remove the flash light from his glove compartment, ran to the rear of the Volkswagen to make a carburetor adjustment.

Lights began to appear, first in the ranch house, then at the barn, "They're on to us." Gray shouted. "Crank up and get out of here, John." He and the Jackson brothers laid low in an orchard until 4:00 AM then infiltrated their way back to Gray's car. By agreement, they would all meet at Gray's home in Richfield.

Chapter 24

The morning sun came up over Red Mountain, its rays piercing every inch of Birmingham's red soil. Gerald arose early, made a pot of coffee and took it to the sundeck at the rear of his home. A few minutes later, Dot appeared, still in her housecoat, to join him. She pulled the coat tight. It was a bit chilly in Birmingham in October. She talked about the upcoming Alabama Fair to show in Birmingham in only a few days, how the plants in the backyard had grown well through the summer. There was a period of total quietness before John posed a question. "Do you honestly think I should let her leave?" Tears welled in his eyes.

Dot despised Megan at the moment. "Let her go, Gerald. She's an inconsiderate, selfish little bitch."

He could hardly believe Dot, "But, Megan is your daughter, Dot, she isn't well."

With utter contempt Dot scolded, "For God sakes, Gerald, wake up and smell the roses! If Megan wants to live with a polygamist, let her go."

He despised the thought, "But she's your own flesh

and blood, Dot. You would throw her out? You'll never see her again."

Dot went for more coffee. "Can I bring you a refill?"

She returned, scolded him for putting her in such a position. "No one could love a daughter more, Gerald. I gave her my life while she was growing up; she was my every prayer, my darling little girl, but Megan....is a disappointment." She looked into the morning sky, choking back tears, "She's lost her sense of values, in fact, I'm not sure she is drug free."

Gerald began to shake his head, "No, no, I refuse to believe Megan would dive to the pits of hell. She's too intelligent to take drugs."

Dot got out of her chair, walked to the end of the porch, poured the remainder of her coffee on the lawn below, turned and looked into Gerald's eyes. "Let her go, Gerald. It's hard love, nothing more, nothing less. If Megan loves you and her children, she'll find her way back."

After breakfast, Gerald called Megan to the bedroom, closed the door. Megan said nothing; stood near the bedroom window waiting. He asked if she realized what she was doing to their family; she merely gave a nod.

"You can catch a plane for Salt Lake City today." He opened his wallet and handed her plane fare. "Take whatever you want, but not the children." He looked into her eyes. "They're no longer yours."

Tears began to stream down her face, she shook her head, "But the children are mine, Gerald. Please don't take them away."

He got to his feet, moved to the door, "I'm not. You're giving them up, Megan. My children are not going to a cult society; bet your ass on it." His anger frightened her, "You be gone when I get home for lunch."

"Gerald, please? I must take my children," she cried. "I must take them, I must."

"No, Megan. They are mine as well. The issue is non-negotiable."

He put on his coat, left her standing near the window, and went into the kitchen. Dot was feeding the children breakfast. He kissed them goodbye and walked to the door, "Dot, watch after them, they are not going to Arizona, I'll be home for lunch."

Dot nodded, "Should I take her to the airport?"

"I think not. Let her call a cab." He left, heart broken. He thought of John, wondered if he would ever return to the ranch.

John sped from Wilson's ranch northwest in a direction he thought would take him to highway 59. A dust cloud appeared at a distance behind him. John's Volkswagen picked up speed, but he realized the cloud of dust was coming closer. He estimated Josh to be two miles back. Miles down the road, John spotted a blockade across the main road. He dismounted the Volkswagen, moved the blockade across the detour opening blocking the road to traffic. He took the actual detour that led to the original road located on the opposite side of the uranium mine. Josh and his men, unaware of John's scheme, continued on the unblocked road toward disaster.

Two hours later, a busy highway appeared, cars going north and south. He came to an entrance ramp, a sign read *To Hurricane.* Gray's home was only a few miles away.

Friday morning, October 30th, John ate breakfast with Gray, the Jackson brothers and Gray's wife, thanked them again for their assistance, kidded the Grays about showing good southern hospitality. Gray smiled for the first time since John had known him. "My friend, we grow cotton here in Utah."

John packed his suitcase; placed it in the backseat and said goodbye. Four days and many road miles later, he came into the city limits of Birmingham. It was a cold dreary day; the place was filled with industrial smoke, lingering like clouds over the city. He checked his watch; the time was now 11:40 AM. Traffic would be buzzing around Britney's place. He decided to call Gerald's office, invite him to lunch. They agreed to meet at Britney's at 12:30 PM.

They took a seat in their favorite place near the front window, John chose a chicken salad sandwich and a small salad; Gerald had the same. A waitress brought them coffee to drink.

"You look thinner." Gerald commented. "What on earth have you been doing all this time?" He asked, a grin appearing on his face.

John, looked out the window, sipped the hot coffee, surveyed the customers in the building then shook his head, "It's a long story, yes, a long story." He quickly changed the subject." "How are Megan and the kids?"

Gerald's look took John aback. "The children are fine, thank you for risking your life to find them."

John wanted to hear more. He reluctantly asked about Megan. Gerald told him of her returning to Arizona. The children at the moment were home with Dot. He planned to take them to the ranch for the week-end.

"Did Dot try to stop her?"

"Heavens no, Dot recommended I let her go." He frowned, "It wasn't easy, but I'll survive. I doubt she'll try stealing the children again."

They finished their meal, walked outside to the parking lot; said their goodbyes. John shouted from across the parking lot. "Call your mother; tell her I'm on my way home."

Gerald waved, opened his car door. "You owe me for a phone call."

South bound traffic on highway 280 was slow this time of day. John turned left at Childersburg, headed for Winterboro. Arriving before school turned out, he traveled over Morrisville Mountain to Nolen's Ranch at the foot. His watch told him Sheila would be at the clinic; he decided to stop, let her know he had arrived.

He entered the clinic to find her busy with a small animal. She looked up then returned to the animal. Moments later, she finished, washed her hands and came to John's side. For once, she actually smiled at him. He felt the pleasure; God it was great to be home. He looked into her beautiful eyes thinking how he loved her, how wrong it would be to reveal his secret.

"John Randall?" She smiled ran into his arms, "You brought my grandchildren home; thank you."

Her touch sent signals to his scarred brain; she belonged to him once. His heart told him to love her, his judgment said to let her go.

"Let's celebrate over dinner this evening." Her eyes melted his will to say no.

He accepted, not sure of his decision. "Mr. Garcia might not approve."

She looked toward Morrisville Mountain, ducked her head for a moment. "No, but it doesn't matter, we're friends, celebrating. Nolen is in his own world. I'm not sure he knows I'm alive. We have much to discuss."

John, feeling dirty, needing a bath, assured her he would be there.

"We'll have dinner at seven."

"Ma'am, thanks for the invitation."

John dressed for the evening; got in his Volkswagen and proceeded up the driveway to Sheila's. He knocked on the door; Lori Garcia answered. She invited him into the living room and offered him a glass of wine. Moments later Sheila came through the door in casual evening dress. She came to his side and offered her hand; John awkwardly took it. "I hope you like roast beef and potatoes, John. Lori is the best cook and this is her favorite." She walked to the fireplace to put on a stick of wood; John rushed to do it for her.

She offered him a seat; Lori would have dinner on the table soon as her rolls were done. "I can't thank you enough for what you have done for my family, John."

He looked at the chandelier hanging from the ceiling, "Ma'am, Gerald is like my own son. He was devastated while those kids were gone." He sipped the wine, "I'm sorry Megan's gone off the deep end."

She paused, reluctant to talk about Megan, not sure Gerald would approve. "I would like for the children to come here, but I'm not sure Gerald will agree." She went to the bar in the dining area to refill their glasses. Returning she looked into his eyes, "John, will you be available to take a ride tomorrow morning about ten?"

His eyes focused on hers, "Where to, Ma'am?"

"You once said you'd like to visit Gerald's cemetery sight; I'd be privileged to take you there."

After dinner, John thanked Sheila and congratulated Lori on a wonderful meal. Checking his watch, it was near 9:00 PM. He said goodnight and turned to Sheila, "Sheila, I'll be at the barn with Bubba when you get ready to go to the cemetery."

She nodded; a slight smile appeared on her face. "Goodnight, John."

At 8:45 AM, near the barn, Sheila blew the horn. John stepped from the doorway. "Bubba, I'm going with Dr. Garcia. We'll be back within the hour."

Sheila drove north over Morrisville Mountain until she arrived at the road leading to the downtown area. She drove past the ball park, rounded a curve, the Company Store came in sight. Before she arrived at the Company Store she turned left across the railroad, bore to the right and drove until she spotted an oval gateway to the cemetery. It appeared to be run down, the man who kept the place died in the summer and the mill had not hired a new grounds keeper. She pulled into the gate then dismounted. "We'll walk in from here." She stepped to his side; he held her arm along the rough trail that led to the back of the cemetery. There in an area designated for fallen soldiers she moved to his tomb. "He lies here, died so young." She began to pull weeds off his grave, John joined in her efforts.

"Was Gerald born before his father was killed?"

"No, in fact, I was alone when Gerald was born. My mother and I never got along, poor thing; she died a tragic death, buried over there by my father."

John asked if they could leave. He didn't feel well. His guilt had mounted in his soul. His mind kept saying you must tell her the truth, his heart said no; she has her own life.

"Do you feel better since you've seen his grave?" Sheila asked.

"No, in fact, I'm frustrated since I can't recall the circumstances."

She drove over Morrisville Mountain south the ranch, up the driveway and down to the barn. "You and Bubba try and get over to that cemetery and clean off his grave. He's Gerald's father and I owe it to him."

John thanked her, assuring her the task would be accomplished. She left him standing near the barn's doorway, he waved, his heart hurting, his mind spinning; he realized what he had to do....

Silent Courage

Chapter 25

First week of December, 1988....

John looked up from the fence he was mending. A black sedan, creating dust, was coming toward him along the fence line. Was his mind playing tricks?

The sedan pulled to a stop, its Utah tag grabbed John's attention. Bubba looked at John. "You know him?"

"Yes, Bubba." John got to his feet; brushed his hands on his trousers. "It's Gray Wolf." John walked toward the sedan, "Gray? How did you find me?"

Gray reached for John's hand. "I found Gerald." Looking toward Morrisville Mountain then the morning sky, Gray wasn't sure how to begin. "Nice mountains, good looking red soil, lots of grass. Bet you raise some fine cattle."

John stared at Gray Wolf. "Yes, but, Gray, you didn't come all the way from Utah to talk about cattle. What brings you here?"

Gray looked across Mahee Creek. He brought his eyes to rest on John's. "The girl's in trouble."

"You drove from Utah to tell me that? Why didn't you use the telephone?"

The Indian removed his hat, brushed his graying hair from his eyes. "Ruby says, Wilson's son to the Underground; she couldn't risk a call."

John put on his work gloves; returned to the fence. "Ruby sent for me? Can't the Underground get her out?"

"Ruby says it's too risky. They'll kill her."

John directed Bubba to pull the wire tight against the post. "Where is she, Gray?"

Gray leaned on the sedan's fender; folded his arms. "She's in a correctional camp. Ruby wouldn't say."

John took a deep breath, his eyes fixed on the fence. He pounded in a staple. "Okay, Gray. What's our next move?"

Bubba interrupted. "Mr. John, it ain't yo move. Ms. Sheila says you ain't going no place."

John ignored Bubba's comment. "Gray, go back to Birmingham. Check in at the Bankhead. Call Gerald; have him meet us for dinner. I'll see you around seven tonight."

Bubba slammed the hammer into the ground. "You is hard headed, Mr. John. You know Ms Sheila's gonna be pissed."

Gray Wolf laughed, backed away, turned toward the main highway. At the end of Sheila's driveway, he turned north...

At lunch time, John led the way to his front porch. Bubba was quiet until Sheila's jeep appeared. "She gotta know, Mr. John."

"Bubba? Keep out of this! I'll face her in time."

Sheila stopped only to let them know Cowboy Mitchell would be at the ranch at 3:00 PM to pick up six of the yearlings.

John found the late evening highway 280 traffic heavier; people returning home from work. He pulled into the Bankhead parking lot and locked his car. Inside, he found Gray Wolf and Gerald stepping from the elevator. "You guys ready for dinner?"

They merged in the center of the room. John turned to them. "Why not eat in the dining room?"

Gerald agreed. They waited a moment to be seated. John asked for a corner table near the back.

After dinner, over coffee, the subject of Megan's return surfaced; John wanted Gerald's thoughts. Gray Wolf listened, but interrupted. "Ruby needs an answer, John."

Gerald nodded, looked at Gray, then at John. "Is Megan ready to come home?"

Gray Wolf wasn't sure. Ruby had not talked to Megan.

"I know Ruby is concerned about the girl's safety."

"Do you want her back?" John asked.

Gerald, filled with frustration, mulled the thought. Problems of the past surfaced his mind. He thought of Dot's refusal to support Megan when she decided to leave.

"Think of your children, Gerald. Have they missed their mother?" John's eyes fixed on Gerald's.

"Yes, Trey cries for her a lot. I agree Meg should be home with our children."

John nodded, looked at Gray Wolf. "Okay, that settles the issue. Tell Ruby I'll be there in a few days."

"John, Mother won't approve of you leaving the ranch again." Gerald frowned. "Maybe I should go."

John looked a Gray, a half smile appeared, he shook his head. "No, Gerald, not your thing. I'll handle it." He sipped the coffee, a frown appearing. "Bubba can manage for a week or so; Sheila? She'll just have to understand."

Gerald looked at Gray. "You think your friend can find Megan?"

Gray nodded, his black eyes squinting. "Ruby? She'll find her all right."

Their meeting ended, John drove back to the ranch. Gerald returned to his office and Gray Wolf went to his rooms with plans to leave Birmingham at an early hour.

John ate breakfast early; checked the kitchen calendar. It would take a couple of days to drive the Volkswagen to Richfield. Could he count on help from the Jackson brothers? Good ole Ruby; she'd have a team ready. He could count on Gray Wolf.

At 7:00 AM John rang Sheila's doorbell. She came to the door dressed for the day. He looked into her eyes, needed her approval to leave for Utah, but assured she would object. "Dr. Garcia, there's something we must discuss."

Sheila opened the door; invited him in. "Could I get you a cup of coffee?" she asked.

"No, Ma'am. I'll only be a minute." His nervous manner alerted Sheila.

"What's the problem, John?"

"Ma'am, it's not a ranch problem." He paused, looking at the floor. "It's your grandchildren. They need their mother. I've learned she's in serious trouble."

Sheila eyes narrowed, she took a deep breath, began to shake her head. "I appreciate your concern, Mr. Randall, but you are interfering in a matter that's none of your business."

John's eyes squinted, a frown appeared, "Sorry, Ma'am, I mean no offense. Gerald is concerned about her safety."

Sheila got up from the couch, moved to the fireplace,

her temper flared. "Gerald is my concern, Mr. Randall, not yours. His wife chose to run off to live with a polygamist and Gerald would take her back?"

John got to his feet, moved toward the door. He turned to look at her. "Sheila, at times, you're impossible. I'll be in the north pasture today." He stepped to the porch, she followed.

"I'm leaving tomorrow for Utah."

She slammed her foot to the floor. "Dam it, John Randall, you dare not leave this ranch again."

John went to the barn; Bubba Miller waited. They drove to the north pasture. Before noon, it began to drizzle. They gathered their tools and returned to the barn. John told Bubba of his plans. Bubba reluctantly agreed to watch after the ranch and the cattle. The day ended, John returned home and packed his bag. He dialed Gerald's number at home. "Will you be in the office tomorrow?"

Gerald nodded, eager to hear John's plan. "I'll be in around nine. I have to be in court at ten."

After a long pause, "I'll be there at 8:30. Can you come in early?"

"See you then."

The phone went dead. John went to bed early. Tomorrow would be a long day. He'd have to reach Oklahoma City before he stopped for the night. He thought of Megan, how much she meant to Gerald, but more importantly, the children needed their mother.

John arrived in Richfield just at day break. He cut the lights and pulled into Gray Wolf's driveway, locked the doors. Suddenly, a tap on the driver's window waked him. Gray Wolf motioned him to come inside. "You've been up all night?"

"Yes, dead for some sleep."

"Go to bed. I'll wake you in a while."

Near 11:00 AM, John felt the touch of a hand on his shoulder; Gray Wolf stood over him. "Ruby's here."

John dressed and went to the kitchen, Wolf's wife handed him a cup of hot coffee. Ruby got to her feet. "Glad you're here, John."

John took a seat, his tired body needed more rest. Wolf's wife brought his breakfast. "Where is she, Ruby?"

Ruby asked if he recalled Molly at the prison near the uranium mine. "Yes, I recall. Megan is there?"

Ruby shook her head. "No, but Molly is no longer at the prison. Wilson had her moved to his correctional camp north."

John looked up. "North, Ruby?"

"Yes, in the desert, the camp is north of the mine."

"You have a plan, Ruby?" John asked.

Ruby looked at the ceiling, shaking her head. "John, for once, I'm baffled. Do we inherit this girl's troubles? Molly says Wilson is hell bent on breaking her will. She refuses to accept his teachings."

"But what happens if she refuses to return to Birmingham?" John frowned, his words carrying a tone of doubt. "What if we risk our butts to rescue her and she turns on us?"

Ruby raised her brow. "It's a possibility. However, Molly says she's like a frightened child." She closed her eyes, taking a weary breath. "I don't know Megan, but, having been there, I feel her pain."

John tipped his head back then looked at Gray. "Would you be receptive to our questioning her here?"

Gray nodded. "Megan once lived in my brother's house."

Ruby interrupted. "Gray, we'll bring her here for questioning only."

"Okay, but not to live, house too small," Gray emphasized.

John got up from the table; poured a second cup of coffee. "Ruby, can you communicate with Molly?"

Ruby nodded. "Yes, but it's risky. I see her once a week." She looked over the table at John. "She comes to Hurricane to buy food for the camp."

John forked his finger through his thinning hair. "Suppose there's a possibility of Megan coming along to help?"

"And put Molly's life on the line? Hell no, John. Not on your life."

Gray's mouth formed a downward turn; he shook his head. "Ruby's right. But we'll find a way."

"And you have a plan, Gray?"

Gray glanced over at John then turned away. "I'm thinking. We have to remember not to row too close to the rocks."

John almost smiled. "It's near noon, Gray, and we still don't have a plan."

Ruby suggested they wait until she could talk to Molly. Maybe Molly could find a way to probe Megan's mind. But Molly must handle the subject with care; she too could become a victim.

They separated with intentions to return to Gray Wolfs home by 8:00 PM the following night. John would get some sleep, Gray Wolf would find the Jackson brothers and Ruby would contact Molly. At their next meeting they would develop a plan to rescue Megan from her web, if Megan was receptive to returning home.

Wednesday evening at 8:00 PM, John arrived at Gray Wolf's to find Ruby and the Jackson brothers behind closed doors. He took his seat at the table, a discussion was in progress.

"John, to bring you up to date, Molly says Megan is becoming weaker everyday. She refuses to worship with Stanley's workers and they refuse to provide her with food."

Gray Wolf cleared his throat, stood; hooked his hand to his hips. "Ruby, you must contact Molly again. Is it possible right away?"

"No, Gray, she will not come to Hurricane again until the day after tomorrow." She paused to ask, "Is that too late?"

Gray cautiously proposed a plan. He explained his plan was not set in concrete, it could be changed, but if successful it could accomplish the mission. They would remove Megan by stealing her away. If the plan worked Megan could be rescued without incident. Megan's cooperation was essential. Gray began to unfold his thoughts on how the plan would work.

Megan will fake an illness, become so sick they have to remove her from the camp to Hurricane Hospital. In route we will construct a roadblock; stop the ambulance and take Megan. "Sounds simple, but it could fail." Gray paused, looking at each one present. "If it fails, she could die. So, we must succeed."

John, feeling the impact of Gray's remark, turned to Ruby. "Insist Molly prepare Megan for this sickness act." He frowned looking at the floor, shaking his head. "We must get Megan away from that maniac."

Friday evening, Megan refused to go to dinner, complaining with an upset stomach. The guards on duty encouraged, she refused. Molly built her ailment in the minds of the guards. Megan was developing a virus; a serious condition. Molly directed Megan be watched.

Near the same hour Megan began to complain with an upset stomach, John Randall, Gray and the Jackson brothers stole a road block for future use.

Near midnight, Megan became worse; she wailed with pain, vomited, her face in agony. A nurse appeared. She checked her blood pressure, temperature, turned to see Molly staring at her. "Ma'am, this girl will die unless we can get her to the hospital."

"Shall we call for an ambulance?" Molly asked.

Moments later, Megan was lifted from her bed, placed on a gurney. The ambulance driver hurriedly headed toward Hurricane. The LPN on duty said no more, but looked at Molly. Megan would soon be under Ruby's control, out of the grips of a mad man.

On the desert road toward Hurricane, the ambulance moved with difficulty. The road was built of packed sand. Near mid-night, the driver pulled to a halt. The road ahead seemed to end; a road block sat across the main road. The driver got out to remove it when suddenly a blast of gun fire sounded in the night air. From behind a sand dune, Gray Wolf and the Jackson brothers appeared. John Randall remained behind the sand dune to act as a back up. If a second vehicle followed the ambulance, John had been instructed to open fire. Gray and the Jackson brothers' must be afforded time to react. Gray quickly opened the ambulance's rear door and lifted a weak Megan to the ground. He carried her to John's Volkswagen, placed her inside and John sped north toward the main highway. The Jackson brothers deflated the ambulance tires, tied the driver's hands and feet; tossed him on the gurney in the ambulance. They quickly crawled into Gray's sedan and the three fled north east leaving the ambulance in the middle of the road.

John, with Megan at his side took highway 69 north and soon arrived in Richfield. John said only a few words enroute; Megan cried softly, eventually falling asleep. John would not wake her until he pulled into Gray Wolf's driveway. Gray's wife came to meet them. Megan waked, looked at John, her eyes red, her body showing signs of hunger. "John, I can't believe you would do this for me."

John said nothing until they were inside Gray's home with the door closed. Ruby was waiting. She put her arms around Megan. "You hungry?" she asked.

Megan, wiping tears, began to nod. "Yes, Ma'am."

Gray Wolf's wife prepared Megan scrambled eggs with toast, and fried bacon.

Gray and the Jackson brothers arrived; came inside. Megan got to her feet; held out her arms to embrace and thank them. She said little, holding back tears, realizing she was no longer at the correctional camp; no longer in the custody Wilson's clan. Ruby's underground had saved her life; an act she would never forget.

Chapter 26

Thursday morning, after breakfast at Gray Wolf's home, Megan removed her clothes, put on Gray Wolf's wife's house coat. She washed and dried her clothes, the only belongings she brought from the camp. In her destitute condition, she kept her mind active, talking to Ruby and Gray's wife about the cruelty she had gone through.

Gray got up from the breakfast table, put on his hat, pushed it away from his eyes and called to John. "Let's walk." He started for the door; John followed.

Gray led the way to a path along the bank of the river, a clean sand filled path Gray walked most days when weather permitted. The morning sun had risen, bright sun rays cast their heat toward the earth. Gray pointed toward the canal with great pride; his family was a member of the canal corporation. "When will you be returning?" Gray asked.

"Soon, may be this afternoon." He tossed a rock toward the river. "Need to get back; Sheila needs me."

"But you came here against her will." Gray almost

smiled, nodded his head. "Damn women. They can be difficult to understand."

John grinned at Gray's comment, kept his eyes on the trail. "But Sheila and I share mutual loved ones; Gerald and the children."

Before noon, John took Megan shopping, bought her necessities to make the trip home, returned to Gray's home to say goodbye. Before leaving John and Megan made a short thank you visit to Ruby.

Leaving Hurricane, they drove until early morning, spending four hours at a Comfort Inn near Oklahoma City. Megan took the bed, John slept on the couch. By 7:00 AM, they ate breakfast, topped off the Volkswagen's tank and headed for Birmingham.

Near sun down the city came in sight. John looked at Megan, her tired eyes smiled. "You ready for this?" he asked.

"No, but I have to face it, John." Tears flowed, she wiped them away. "Stupidity can make us do crazy things." She turned in her seat to face him. "I feel so free, John, thanks to you."

John kept focused on the heavy traffic on I-65. He turned on I-59 toward Gadsden. "Where are you taking me?"

"We're going to the farm, Meg."

"May I ask, why?"

"I think it would be better for you and Gerald to have some time together before you see the children." He paused. "Let's mend the fences one at a time, okay?"

She smiled for the first time since leaving the correctional camp. "John Randall? You're a true friend. Do you plan to return to the ranch?"

"It depends. Sheila can be difficult and I left for Utah without her approval."

"John, I feel terrible. You risked losing your job to rescue me." Megan frowned, shaking her head. "What an inconsiderate ungrateful, spoiled, immature idiot I've been."

"At times, it takes adversity to wake us up, Meg." John led the way to the living room; built a fire and called Gerald.

"How can I face him after what I've done?"

"With honesty, Megan. We're all prone to error, no one is perfect."

"But he couldn't love me after my abandoning my children." She started to cry. "I'm no good, John, plain no good."

John put a second log on the fire. "Never doubt your self worth, Meg. You're important in the lives of two lovely children." He frowned. "So get your act together. You showed great strength of character, not accepting Wilson's religion. You didn't yield to his dominance."

A car pulled into John's driveway and moments later, a slight knock came at the door. John opened it; Gerald stepped inside; looked at Megan. "Good evening, Megan." He nodded. "Welcome home."

Megan, shook her head, keeping her eyes focused on his, hardly knowing what to say. "Gerald, I've been such a fool, but I promise you, I haven't broken our marriage vows."

John was taken aback. How could she make such a comment after living in the same household with a polygamist for months? John's will to keep her honest bounced forward. "Megan, please...be honest with Gerald."

Megan, her eyes remained on Gerald's frown at John's comment. "I am being honest, John." She wiped tears from her eyes. "Not once did I go into that man's bedroom. I tried to make myself, but I couldn't." She fought back tears. "I found his religion repulsive. He tried to force me to teach his ideas to the young; I refused. Our relationship deteriorated before the end of my first day."

Gerald listened, not sure she was telling the whole truth, not sure she wasn't. "But how could you leave Stacey and Trey, Megan?"

"I was so immature I didn't understand what I was doing. I've paid for what I've done. I've lived through hell."

Gerald took a deep breath, exhaled. "What's happen to Melanie?"

"She's a thing of the past; thank God. I'm a whole person now; I'm sure of it."

"Are you sure you're ready to come home and be a mother?"

She nodded, eyes filled with tears. "I'll make it up to you, Gerald; I promise."

Gerald moved to the foyer, picked up the telephone, called his home number, Megan's mother answered.

"Dot, Meg is back, I'm bringing her home."

After a long paused, Gerald heard a soft sigh. "Has she come to her senses?"

"I'm sure of it. Have the children wait dinner. They'll be surprised at our dinner guest."

The streets of Sylacauga were crowded with mostly women buying Christmas gifts, shopping for specialties in small shops along Main Street. Sheila thought how quickly time had passed. Nolen would be home to stay in a couple of weeks. She would hold him to his promise. Finishing her shopping she left for home wondering what John was doing. Why was she concerned with what he was doing? Why was he in her thoughts every moment of every day? She was beginning to regret bringing him to the ranch. But now that he's run off to Utah without her sanction, it would be a good time to sever their relationship. But she needed John. And then, there was something about John Randall that disturbed her; he was more than a ranch hand. She sat on the veranda, looked at the moon in the sky, wondering where Nolen was tonight, but most of all, she wondered if John Randall would return.

Suddenly, the telephone rang in the foyer. Sheila jumped to her feet, ran to pick up the receiver...

The voice made cold chills run up her spine. "Ma'am, this is John Randall. I'm back." He paused. "Am I fired? I apologize for leaving without your concurrence." He closed his eyes, took a weary breath. "But Ma'am, I'd be a liar if I said I'm sorry I brought Meg home."

Sheila's heart pounded. She tried to use her business voice, but in reality wanted to see him, now. "John Randall, you're impossible. How could you go the Utah against my wishes?"

"Ma'am, I'm guilty as charged. Should I bring the house key by on my way out?"

She paused, wanting to invite him up, knowing well, she shouldn't. "No. I need you here, but, John, no more trips to Utah." She hesitated, he felt her long pause. "Bubba's been missing you."

"Good man, Ma'am."

"Lori has fixed vegetable soup. We'll wait dinner on you. I want you to tell me about Megan."

December 15....

Sheila turned the television off after mid-night, her mind filled with thoughts of Stacey and Trey reunited with their mother in Birmingham. After breakfast, she dressed for work then she flipped on the morning news. An announcer on NBC stated three men were found in a uranium pit in an Arizona Desert area. They suffered heat exposure and hunger from days in the pit.

Flicking off the set, she asked Lori to pick up the mail; have any calls transferred to the clinic. She mounted the jeep as John's vehicle pulled into the yard, she waited....

"Sheila, I'm going to the cemetery to clean off Gerald's grave. I should be back in a couple hours."

She nodded, cranking the jeep, "Put down hay before you leave."

He looked at her, his desires mounting, aware he couldn't remain at Nolen's Ranch much longer.

John and Bubba pulled into the cemetery; took sling blades and began to cut high weeds from Gerald's grave site. Thirty minutes later, the two men moved to the shade of a tree, John opened two ice cold soft drinks he had brought from home. Perspiration dripped from Bubba's face. He took a deep breath, "Did you actually know Mr. Gerald?" He asked, his dark eyes piercing John's.

John looked at Bubba recalling their friendship long

before he left for the war in the early fifties, remembering how Bubba lost a leg in Korea. "Why do you ask, Bubba? Do you doubt I knew the man?"

Bubba shook his head, looked at John with a frown, "Yeah, but Mr. John, something ain't right, can't put my finger on it, but something just ain't right."

John looked across the graves and fields to the south, the roar of the cotton mill brought tears to his eyes. His father and mother had worked in that cotton mill when he was a boy; he had old friends here, but his situation locked him out. He was a prisoner in his own world. "Bubba, it's a long story, one I'll have to take to my grave."

Bubba looked at John, "That's foolish. Mr. John, you needs some of yo' own counseling, man. You can talk to me, man. I'm yo' friend. This ain't Japan."

John walked to the truck, placed the swing blades in the bed, "Bubba, did you attend Gerald's funeral?"

Bubba eyed John, carefully observing his moves. "I was here for a funeral, all right, but I'm not so sure it was Mr. Gerald's."

John nodded. "Why would you doubt it? You know damn well caskets from a war zone aren't opened, Bubba." He glared a convincing look.

"Can't we sit awhile, Mr. John?" Bubba pulled a twig from the tree, began to pick his teeth, "I'm not sure Mr. Gerald is dead, Mr. John."

John began to shake his head, "That's absurd, Bubba. He's been buried here for 37 years."

Bubba's eyes were fixed on John's. He pointed toward the grave. "But that ain't Mr. Gerald. You know it ain't him."

John frowned, "I wouldn't go expressing that thought to Dr. Garcia, Bubba." He glanced at the grave. "It would frustrate her if she thought he wasn't here."

"Yes, Sir, I'll remember to mind my own business." Bubba got to his feet and moved to the passenger's side of the truck. "But, Mr. John, Something just ain't right."

John and Bubba arrived at the barn, fed the younger yearlings, put the brood cows into the near pasture. John's day was going well until Dr. Garcia showed up with a disgusting attitude. She reminded John of the Sheila he met the day he came to buy cattle; frustrated, unhappy with the world. "Sheila, you're not yourself...what gives?" John frowned.

She choked back tears, "What is it to you, John Randall?"

Relegated to his place, an employee he lowered his head, felt the wrath of her reprimand. It cut deeply into his soul. "Sorry, Dr. Garcia, I didn't mean to upset you." He turned to leave, calling Bubba to follow. She gained her composure, and called to him, "John, I didn't mean to hurt you." She wiped her eyes. "I'll talk to you later."

He later learned she was in the throes of an argument with Nolen. He had decided he no longer cared for the life he had in a small town. He preferred living in a larger city, associating with the elite, even rubbing shoulders with the governor.

Nolen had made a drastic change. Sheila suspected an affair, but he wouldn't admit it. She thought of mid-life changes; he was in his fifties. Lori couldn't talk about it; she knew little about Nolen. Sheila suggested marriage counseling, he refused. "Sheila, I'll give you the ranch and the clinic. The remainder of our assets will be negotiated by an attorney. Sorry, Sheila, I wouldn't be happy here any longer."

"But, Nolen, we have a son. You're being selfish."

Nolen breathed deeply, "He's grown and gone, I'm not concerned about Ben. He has his own life; I have mine."

"What about our marriage vows, you feel no obligation?"

"Come on, Sheila, this is 1988 not 1900; people divorce everyday."

"I have nothing further to say, Nolen. You'll hear from my attorney."

Before November 15th, Lori packed her things and moved to Montgomery. She wasn't happy with Nolen's decision, but had no choice. She couldn't live on Joe's retirement.

Gerald negotiated the divorce settlement. It became permanent on December 6, 1988. Sheila agreed to the settlement. Thelma Miller, Bubba's sister came to live in the servant quarters. Thelma, now married, had no children. She assumed the responsibility for keeping Sheila's home in good order. Sheila had plans for Thelma to assume the role of a nanny for Stacey and Trey.

Chapter 27

December 1988....

With Christmas fast approaching, Sheila wasn't the same. Though she disapproved of Nolen's behavior; not sure she loved him anymore, he continued to surface her mind. Christmas would be different without him, but she refused to live the rest of her life grieving over Nolen Garcia. She'd blot him out of her mind; erase him from her memory.

The week before Christmas, John surprised Sheila with a gift. She placed the center piece on her dining room table. She thanked him, keeping her mind on a single thought. John Randall was edging closer, trying to take over as the head of her family; should she resent it, or respect him for it? He reminded her of Gerald, but how would she know? Gerald had been gone thirty years.

A few days before Christmas, John came home from work, took a bath and turned on the television. The phone rang in the foyer...

The voice was mellow; he'd heard it before, but where?

With a puzzled mind he wouldn't venture to guess. "Sorry I can't put a name to your voice."

She laughed, "You shouldn't try." The caller said, "I'm a female friend from Utah."

John's heart melted. "You're Ruby?"

"Yes, in Birmingham. I must see you."

"You are actually in Alabama, Ruby?"

"Yes, John. My position with the Underground is compromised. Wilson knows what I've been doing. It was either leave Utah or wind up in a desert grave."

"Have you checked in?"

"No, I'm at the airport. Could you help me?"

"I'm an hour away, Ruby. I'll call my friend, Gerald. You remember Megan and the children. If Gerald's in town, he'll take you to his home until I can arrange to get there."

John heard a sigh of relief, "Thank you, John. I'll wait here."

John dialed Gerald's office number, arranged for Dot Sutton to take Ruby to his home.

John drove up the driveway to Sheila's home; Bubba called her home the "Big House." John knocked; Sheila came to the door in jeans and blouse. "Ruby's in trouble, Sheila. We have to help."

Sheila peered deeply into his eyes. "Ruby, you mean the lady from Utah? She came here to ask for your help?"

"Yes, her Underground position was compromised." He frowned, shaking his head, "Wilson has no mercy; a religious nut."

Sheila moved closer, took a seat next to him, took his hand in hers. "Could it be she wanted more?"

John, frustrated, looked into her eyes, his heart saying caress her; his mind wouldn't allow it. "Ruby needs help, nothing more." His words were reassuring, she got to her feet. "Then bring her here."

John walked toward the door, looked into darkness, the shadow of the barn stood taller than Morrisville Mountain. He stepped to the porch, turned with burning desire, but said no more. He'd visit Amanda Sims tomorrow for a consultation.

Amanda called Sheila with good news; Theodore Gray had sold the Chicago Clinic to his partner. "He will take over Dad's practice next week."

Amanda and her mother were planning Amanda's wedding. Ted had already purchased a home on a hill near the railroad at Syco; a short distance from his practice in Morrisville. Amanda wanted Stacey and Trey to participate in her wedding. "Will Megan mind?"

"Absolutely not. She'll love it. Is Dr. Sims retiring?" Sheila asked.

"Yes, so is Mother, after all these years."

Sheila paused, "Will you be in your office tomorrow?"

Amanda, nodded, "Yes, till noon. What's up?"

"It's personal."

Sheila arrived at Amanda's office near 10:30 AM, parked in the rear, bounded up the steps. Dr. Sims is in the lab, Dr. Garcia; she's expecting you."

Amanda looked up into the eyes of Sheila, "What's so important to make you leave the clinic, Sheila?" She grinned, sticking her hand out.

"Am I intruding at a bad time?"

Amanda frowned. "It's lunch time. Let's go to the cafeteria."

They mounted Sheila's jeep and left for the hospital. Amanda talked incessantly about her upcoming wedding; Sheila wasn't interested at the moment.

They ordered, finished their meal, and Sheila reluctantly began. "Amanda, the subject is not my affair." She frowned. "It's about John Randall. Is there a possibility of correcting those scars?"

Amanda considered the possibilities. "Yes, Ted once told me it could be done."

"I understand you discussed surgery with him years ago."

"Yes, I recommended surgery before Megan went to Chicago."

They rode back to Amanda's office, Sheila cut the engine. They sat for a spell talking about the upcoming wedding. Amanda was excited.

"I must get back to the clinic." Sheila looked at the traffic along Main Street. "Let my visit be our secret. John might resent me discussing his problem."

Amanda, dismounted the jeep, looked into Sheila's eyes. "Don't fret; I'll prompt him to get his face corrected." She moved up the steps, turned, "Is he important to you?"

Sheila looked at her, cranked her vehicle, smiled looking toward Amanda. "What do you think?"

Amanda waved, walked into the office, closed the door. John Randall would be a handsome man when Ted removed those ugly scars.

Sheila returned to the clinic assured Amanda would carry through with her promise. She drove over the mountain, through the valley, crossed the double bridges. John would soon have a new face.

Thursday evening, John sat alone watching television while reading the Birmingham News. The telephone rang; it was Amanda calling. She wanted him to come in the following day for a visit. "Not sure what Sheila has in mind for us tomorrow, Amanda, I'll try." He paused, "Is it important?

"John, believe me, it's in your best interest."

"I'll talk with Sheila, first thing. What time?"

"No rush, near noon? Let's have lunch."

Friday morning after breakfast, John dressed for work, keeping in mind he must talk with Sheila. He and Bubba mended fences along the east end of the ranch for two hours then returned to the barn. "Bubba, I have to go into Sylacauga." He rubbed his hands on his trousers, "Amanda called last night."

He asked Bubba to look after things.

"Mr. John, you ain't running off to Utah agin, is you?"

John laughed. "No, Bubba. No more Utah visits."

John drove to the clinic to inform Sheila he had an appointment in Sylacauga. He took a quick shower, dressed and drove to Amanda's office. She invited him in and closed the door.

With a stern look, Amanda began. "What I have to say is important, Mr. Randall, so take note of it."

"Amanda, will you please cut this formality? I'm John. Why this... Mr. Randall stuff?"

She eyed him, admiring his courage. He'd risked his life to rescue not only Gerald's kids. She smiled at the thought, tossed her pencil on her desk. "Okay, John Randall. It's time you get those scars removed. I have a dear friend who finds it important."

He frowned, shaking his head, "Gerald hasn't mentioned the scars. Why his sudden interest in changing my face?"

"John, you have more than one friend. She closed her eyes, took a weary breath. "I'm not at liberty to tell you the person's name, so, don't ask."

"Is Ted willing to tackle it?" John asked.

Amanda nodded, "Yes, you'll be his first Alabama patient. He'll do the operation here in Sylacauga. I'll be with you as well." She smiled. "Okay?"

John paused, in deep thought, tears welled, "How long will I have to be away from the ranch?"

"Let's discuss it over lunch. I'm hungry."

Mounting Amanda's jeep, they drove to the hospital's cafeteria, pulled into a parking space, found Amanda's favorite table, both ordered soup and salad.

After lunch, Amanda began. "Ted thinks you shouldn't be hospitalized more than a few days." She frowned, thinking of recovery, "Who will look after you when you return home?" she asked.

"Not sure, maybe Ruby, my friend from Utah." He cleared his throat. "She needs work."

"Recovery is important. Can you depend on her?" Amanda asked.

"I'll discuss it with Sheila."

Amanda nodded, "A good idea. Sheila is wise."

Chapter 28

After Christmas, 1988....

Ted scheduled the operation. Before 6:00 AM, John drove to the Sylacauga Hospital; Amanda was waiting. She assisted in John's prep and remained with him until the anesthetist put him under. Four hours later, after extensive surgery, John waked in ICU. He would be there for two days.

Sheila arranged for John to move into a guest bed room. Ruby served as his nurse. Ted kept a close vigil, visiting John at the ranch each week until it was time to remove the bandages. Ruby drove John to the Sylacauga Hospital; Amanda met them at the desk. It would be an eventful day; Sheila came in for the occasion; Ted showed up at mid-morning. John received a lecture, what he could expect, In the presence of Sheila and Amanda, Ted began to peel away the bandages. Ruby stood near, the excitement showing on her chubby face. The bandages gone; the scars were no longer there. The synthetic skin looked no different from John's own. John starred at Sheila, then at Amanda, neither commented. They looked at each other. Ted Gray smiled, "John, you look great." He held a mirror; John looked; tears streamed from his eyes. For the first time in thirty years, he felt whole again; capable of meeting people without hiding his face.

Sheila nodded, a smile appearing on her face, "Ted, he looks like Gerald, Jr."

Amanda laughed, "That's quite an observation, Sheila. I concur; older, but none the less, same features."

Ted stood near John touching the skin near his thin hair line, "Sorry, I can't take credit for that. I only removed the scars."

John returned to work three weeks after the operation. Thelma Miller gave up her job at the ranch to look after her aging mother. Ruby became the new live in nanny and house keeper for Sheila. John returned to his home down near the highway. Gerald continued to spend week ends at the ranch. Close ties soon developed between Gerald's children and John Randall. He insisted Sheila give Trey a new pinto pony for Christmas. Stacey spent many hours listening to John's stories about the islands of Japan.

With Christmas now behind them, Stacey and Trey prepared to return to school in Birmingham. Stacey missed John Randall, spoke of him often; she'd grown to love him for his kindness.

In early January, Amanda called Sylacauga Airport to ask Bunk Nabors to service the Beechcraft. She'd be flying to a meeting in Montgomery. Arriving at Montgomery's airport, she caught a cab to the forensic science building.

The meeting, chaired by Robert Findley, brought the attendees up to date on latest techniques in finger printing cadavers. The meeting ended before 1:00 PM. She had the cab driver stop at Chris' downtown. She grabbed a quick bite to eat, picked up a copy of the Montgomery Advertiser to read on her way back to the airport. On the second page an announcement caught her eye. Nolen Garcia and his new wife were spending their honey moon in Ireland. The couple would return to their home, a renovated mansion on Perry Street.

On the night of January 5th, 1989, near 11:00 PM, a pick-up truck without headlights pulled under an archway at the Morrisville Cemetery. From his truck, the driver removed a marker, placed it in a wheel barrow. By moonlight, he wheeled the marker from a grave and replaced it with the new one. He loaded the old marker on to the truck. Thirty minutes later, the marker taken from Gerald Price's grave was covered with old feed sacks and stored for safe keeping under a front porch.

A week later, Sheila went to the cemetery to remove a dead poinsettia from Gerald's grave. She found something strange, his marker was missing. A new marker stood in its placed, it read, *John Randall lies here. May his soul rest in peace.*

Sheila stood at the grave site and cried. This was not Halloween. What was happening to John Randall's mind? Would he swindle her, steal his way into her family? God forbid. She took the dead plant from the grave, backed away and sped to the ranch. There must be a logical explanation. She pulled the jeep down to barn; Bubba appeared.

"Where's John?" Bubba detected sharpness in her voice.

"Ma'am, don't know, didn't say where he was going."

"I want to see him at the clinic as soon as he returns."

Bubba nodded, Sheila wheeled the jeep in the direction of the clinic.

Near 10:30 AM, January 6th, John pulled into his driveway at the farm near Birmingham. The place had been closed for a while. He'd promised Ruby she could rest a few days at the farm. He hauled in wood for a fire and spent an hour making the place presentable. Ruby would not arrive until after work. She planned to cook a roast duck with the trimmings. John would be her dinner guest.

Before noon, John dialed Gerald's number. The phone rang twice. Gerald was in a meeting. "Would you take a message, please? Tell Gerald, John Randall will be at Britney's at 11:45. It's important I see him."

Amanda's office phone rang. Amanda had gone to the cafeteria for lunch. "This is Dr. Garcia, have her call."

Before stopping work for lunch, Bubba finished putting hay down for the yearlings, and reached for his lunch pail. Following his and John's routine, Bubba walked down to John's front porch to have lunch and to rest. Grass near the right side of the porch had been trampled. Bubba's curiosity mounted. He placed his lunch pail on the porch, crawled underneath. Someone had placed feed sacks over a stone. Bubba pulled the sacks away. It was the marker Ms. Sheila had bought for Gerald's grave. Bubba's mind drifted to the day he and John cleaned off Gerald's grave site. It didn't make sense that Gerald's army friend would remove his old buddy's marker. Before reporting his find to Ms. Sheila, he had to make a visit.

Still on his lunch hour, Bubba drove to the cemetery. The original marker had been replaced. The new marker verified what Bubba felt in his heart for months. The man working with him at the ranch wasn't John Randall. He doubted the Morrisville grave held the remains of Gerald Price. Bubba rushed to the clinic, Dr. Garcia wasn't in.

Silent Courage

Chapter 29

January 8, 1989...

Gerald Price, Jr. joined John at Britney's. They had their usual meal, John seemed distant, quiet, not his normal friendly self. Gerald looked at him, then out the front window, "Okay, what's bothering you, John?"

"My world is falling apart." He shook his head. "I have every reason to be happy now that I no longer resemble Frankenstein."

"Well, why the change in attitude?"

"Not sure you'd want to know."

"Try me. We're friends, you know."

"Ted corrected my face, but who can correct guilt?" he frowned.

"Guilt?" Gerald countered, observing John's emotional state. He was different.

"What's this about, John?" Gerald's eyes trained on John's.

Taking his handkerchief from his pocket, John dried the corner of his eyes. "I'm not sure it's something you'd like to hear." He swallowed hard. "Maybe we should let well enough be."

"Damn it, John! Stop playing games. What's your problem?"

John tugged at the back of his neck, tension caused his temples to ache. "I should have stayed in Japan, but I didn't return to hurt a soul."

Gerald was spell bound, as John told the story of a black American soldier who worked undercover during the Korean War. He died in Korea at the time Gerald Price was wounded. An imposter was selected to pose as John Randall; to protect the identity of the agent. Anoka Faureta worked with both American and Japanese agents. "I'm that imposter, Gerald. I've been known as John Randall for thirty years."

"Hold on, John, you have me on a roller coaster. You're moving too fast." Gerald paused a moment then continued, "If you aren't John Randall, then who the hell are you, man?" Gerald's tension mounted.

"Gerald, I'm not sure you want to know." He got to his feet, "Ruby is waiting for me at the farm." They moved outside, John reached for his hand, "Call your mother and tell her I'm returning to Japan tomorrow. I think it's where I belong."

Gerald nodded, "Okay, but, you haven't answered my question?"

John opened the door to the Volkswagen, hesitated a moment, Gerald deserved an answer. "I'm your greatest fan, your supporter and I love you and the kids as if you were my own."

"But for God sakes, tell me who you are." Gerald raised his voice, shaking his head, evident frustration on his face, "If you are my friend, you owe me the courtesy to tell me your real name."

John Randall paused, "All right. You've made your point." John stared at the ground, not sure he should answer.

Gerald came close, his eyes showing concern, "John, before you go running back to Japan, surely you'll answer this one question for me."

John looked south across Red Mountain, the Vulcan standing like a stalwart guard over the entire city, "Will you agree to not tell a soul until I can leave the country?"

"John Randall, I've known from the day you returned from Japan, you were different. But you're my friend, and my hero."

John ducked his head, looked north toward Cullman, felt the impact of Gerald's remark, wished he could shirk his responsibility, knowing it was time to face facts. "Gerald, I've faced a flamethrower, but nothing compares to this moment in my life. I'm actually nobody. I have returned from the dead, not a citizen of the country. I have no finger prints, no identity, for all purposes, I'm nothing, I am dead."

Gerald held out his hand, "Say no more, please, John, I should have known long ago." Tears welled in Gerald's eyes, "You told me through your actions, through your love for my family." He grabbed John and hugged him. "You have to be my Dad."

John nodded, "Yes, I learned my true identity on my last trip to Japan. I'm Gerald Price, Sr." He held to Gerald, the two embraced. Others leaving the restaurant observed their affection.

"Gerald, Sheila must never be told. I am not worthy of her love."

Gerald nodded, "But Mother needs you, Dad."

Tears welled in John's eyes, for the first time, Gerald called him "Dad."

"Give me until late tomorrow before you tell her." He cleared his throat, tears streaming. Gerald promised.

Gerald left his father in the parking lot. It was time to bring his mother and father together. He'd bring up the subject at Megan's birthday party. Sheila had suggested they meet at the ranch to celebrate on Sunday. Gerald made his plans; John Randall would attend.

Gerald called Ruby at John's farm to invite her and John to the ranch on Sunday to celebrate Megan's birthday. Ruby, not knowing John's desires, promised to call later. If he agreed to attend, she promised to bring a roast duck.

Sunday morning, John and Ruby arrived at the ranch before 11:00 AM. He pulled up beside Gerald's new sports sedan.

Sheila walked to the porch dressed in jeans, her knee length boots gave her a western look. It was Megan's birthday, but Sheila was determined to face John Randall about Gerald's grave marker. Stacey and Trey ran to John, wrapping their arms around his legs.

After they ate Megan's birthday dinner, they presented her with gifts. Gerald proposed a toast to family. Stacey and Trey stuck close to their mother's side.

Afterwards, Sheila walked to the back porch, inviting John, to join her. It was a cold cloudy day, but no wind. "Let's walk to the barn, check on Stacey's pony."

John commented about the aging animal Stacey loved so dearly. "And you must know Trey dearly loves his pinto." He laughed.

She stopped a few steps short of the gate, turned; placed her hands on her hips. "John, why did you remove Gerald's grave marker?"

John, taken aback, took a deep breath, looked skyward; he could no longer pretend. "Sheila, I'm sorry if I've hurt you, but Gerald isn't there; I'm....Gerald."

She glared at John, apparent anger in her eyes, "No way, Mr. Randall, you ungrateful rogue, you thief!" She ran toward the back steps tears streaming from her face. She called to Gerald, "Get this man off my property." She shouted. She ran into her bedroom, closed the door.

Gerald met John at the foot of the steps, "Dad, you told her, what did you say?"

John shook his head, "She accused me of trying to steal my own identity."

Gerald took John by the arm, they walked to the sports sedan, "Let's take a ride."

At the end of the driveway, Gerald turned right, over the mountain, he turned into the road leading to Morrisville, crossed the railroad tracks; drove directly to the cemetery. They walked to the grave site. Gerald read the epitaph, "Did you know Mr. Randall?"

Gerald, Sr., looked into the eyes of his son. "I don't think I ever met him, but I met his parents in Columbus." He paused, pulling a blade of grass from the grave. "I plan to visit them soon."

"What happened to your belongings when you were wounded in Korea?"

Gerald Sr. frowned, "Don't think I ever asked. After my days in the hospital, I was left with one thing; a ring on my finger; a wedding band."

Gerald, Jr., eyes fixed on Gerald, Sr., "And where is it?"

"I've kept it all these years, but, Gerald, it wouldn't matter. Sheila is convinced I'm trying to steal my way into her family." He shook his head, folding his arms, "For years, I didn't know who I was." He looked out the car window. "Now that I know, I'm miserable."

Gerald reached from the driver's seat to touch his father's hand. "Don't worry. The truth of your identity will win; I believe it."

An hour later, Gerald pulled into the driveway. Gerald, Sr. got out, shook his son's hand, asked him to tell Ruby it was time they return to Birmingham.

Ruby and John made conversation on their return trip to Birmingham. She wasn't privileged to the information he and Sheila had shared at the barn. John built a fire and poured them a glass of white wine. She brought in leftovers from the duck, prepared two plates and they ate their supper together. John got to his feet put a stick of oak on the fire. "Ruby, I won't be returning to the ranch job anymore; I'm going back to Japan for a while." He frowned, shaking his head, "Things haven't been going well. I need some time to think."

She gazed at him, nodding with no concept of why he was so unhappy. "John, something is bothering you. Would you like to talk about it? We're friends, you know."

He looked at her, not sure he should reveal family secrets, but knowing she was a friend. "It's a long story; not sure you're ready for it."

She frowned, "John, it couldn't be as complicated as the Underground in Utah."

"Okay,"

"Go ahead. We have time on our hands."

John began with the Korean War. He talked about marrying his high school sweetheart, how he joined the army to serve in Korea. During his army training, his wife got pregnant, had a child after he was supposedly killed in Korea. He told her how he had been wounded by a flamethrower, his face scarred so badly he decided to remain in Japan. The story fascinated Ruby. She sat in awe listening to John, hardly knowing what to say. He completed his story and returned to Sheila and the ranch. Sheila had the child, re-married and eventually divorced; winning the ranch as a part of the settlement.

John finished his story then looked into her eyes. "Sheila is my wife; Gerald is my son; I'm not dead, but since I've found out who I am; I'm miserable." He placed his hands over his eyes. "I came to Colorado City, Ruby, not for Sheila's sake, but for my own. Those kids I wanted to rescue are my grandchildren."

Ruby, knowing the pain John was feeling, refilled their wine glasses and came to his side on the living room couch. "She's a wonderful person, gone through hell rearing your child alone." She frowned, "What do you expect after so many years; a sex party to celebrate your absence? Wake up and smell the roses, man." She lit a cigarette, sipped the wine. "What is the greatest moment you and Sheila shared together as youngsters?"

"Hell, Ruby, my brain has been scrambled; how am I to remember such an event?"

John, if she means anything to you; get your priorities in order; put your mind to work. What was that great event?"

John rubbed his brow, his mind searching for information. Then it came to him, he smiled, "Of course, the hours we spent at lunch time at Mom and Pops restaurant in Sylacauga. Ruby, she loved chocolate syrup on her ice cream."

"Then get off your duffs and call her, right now. Ask her to meet you at Mom and Pops tomorrow for lunch and John, promise not to mention Gerald."

John rebelled, but she insisted. "What is there to lose, John?" She moved to the fireplace to warm her backside. "You're a brave man, John Randall, not a wimp, stand up."

John felt his anger level rise, kept his emotions to himself, grinned like a school boy, looking into Ruby's eyes. "You can be the most aggravating, beautiful bitch

I know, Ruby." He laughed looking into her dark eyes. "And I don't even know your last name."

She left the fireplace, took a seat on the couch. "I prefer you call me Ruby, John. If there is a need for a second name, then you select one."

After the fire died down in the living room, Ruby bade John good night and moved to the back bedroom. John went to his bedroom; picked up the receiver and dialed Sheila....

Megan's birthday party ended. Gerald and his family returned to Birmingham Sunday evening. Sheila was left alone expecting Ruby to return before she had to go to the clinic on Monday. Ruby returned by 8:00 next morning.

At 11:30 Sheila pulled to the curb, walked into Mom and Pops café, her mind whirling with memories of her high school days. Praying Gerald was for real, not sure John Randall wasn't scamming her family she took a seat in a booth she had occupied many times. Moments later the door opened and the man she had known as John Randall came to her table. She looked into his eyes, not sure she wanted to speak; not convinced Gerald could return from the dead. Not to be crude or unfriendly, a trait she had always despised, she forced herself to exchange greetings. John took a seat before calling to the waitress, "Ma'am, can I smoke in here? I used to years ago."

The waitress shook her head, "No more, Sir, it's not permitted now."

Gerald smiled, "Sheila, I can recall when we came here because of my being able to smoke."

Not sure John Randall had not talked to Gerald during their years of service, she looked at him. "Did Gerald tell you about our days here?"

He frowned, "Sheila, how can I convince you I'm for real?"

She gave him a skeptical look then ordered her meal, he ordered his; she turned to the waitress, "Please bring me chocolate ice cream for desert." He interrupted, "And would you please fill it with chocolate syrup?"

Sheila was taken aback. How could he know, tears welled in her eyes, "John, don't do this to me. It's cruel."

He reached for her hand, took the ring he had stored away in his wallet for years and slipped it on his finger, "This is the wedding band you gave me years ago; the one thing I've held on to."

She took the ring in her hand. It was Gerald's all right. She reached for his hand, tears flowing down her cheeks. "Why didn't you return home after the war?"

He held her hand, looking into her eyes, "I can't explain it, but I wasn't capable of thinking, Sheila." He frowned, feeling her pain, his own thoughts choking him. "Sheila, you, Gerald and the children mean more to me than life."

"Welcome home, Gerald." She got up from the table, walked to the cashier; Gerald took the bill from her hand. "Sheila, I'm head of this family." He paid the bill, they stepped outside. She curled her arm in his; they walked toward the jeep. "Incidentally, since Dad died, Mother is all alone. Could we move her into my house on the road?"

"Grand idea, do ask if she'd like to come."

"I'll drive out tomorrow." He took the driver's seat. "She doesn't know I'm back."

"Gerald, what about your car, we didn't come together, remember?"

Gerald laughed. "You think of everything, Sheila. Bubba and I will pick it up in the morning. Let's celebrate today." "Gerald, be careful how you tell your mother. She getting old and she could have a heart attack you know."

"Not, Mom, honey. She's stronger than steel."

Sheila smiled, "Should we go through matrimony again?"

"Not sure it's necessary, but whatever you like, Sheila. You're the boss; I manage the ranch."

She turned in her seat, looked into his eyes. "I think it would be nice if we could manage a honeymoon."

"Good idea." He smiled. "Maybe a cruise some place?"

"Yes, a cruise would be nice." She nodded. "Gerald, do you remember our first honeymoon?"

Keeping his eyes fixed on the road, he thought of that single night they spent together at the Jeff Davis Hotel in Montgomery. "How could I forget?" he smiled. "We only had one night before I had to leave for the Army."

"Yes, but we were so much in love."

"Have we lost that love, Sheila?"

She paused, tears welling in her eyes. "No, since you came back, it seems to grow deeper every day."

He reached for her hand. "We have so much catching up to do. I promise to make up for all that time we were apart."

"What shall we tell the grandchildren?" she asked.

"Why not tell them the truth? After all, we're their grandparents."

2011

Made in the USA